MW00761468

Sour Cream, Blueberries, and You

A Memoir

John Shubeck

iUniverse, Inc.
Bloomington

Sour Cream, Blueberries, and You
A Memoir

Copyright © 2013 John Shubeck

All rights reserved. No part of this book may be used or reproduced by any means, graphic, electronic, or mechanical, including photocopying, recording, taping or by any information storage retrieval system without the written permission of the publisher except in the case of brief quotations embodied in critical articles and reviews.

iUniverse books may be ordered through booksellers or by contacting:

iUniverse
1663 Liberty Drive
Bloomington, IN 47403
www.iuniverse.com
1-800-Authors (1-800-288-4677)

Because of the dynamic nature of the Internet, any Web addresses or links contained in this book may have changed since publication and may no longer be valid. The views expressed in this work are solely those of the author and do not necessarily reflect the views of the publisher, and the publisher hereby disclaims any responsibility for them.

Any people depicted in stock imagery provided by Thinkstock are models, and such images are being used for illustrative purposes only.

Certain stock imagery © Thinkstock.

ISBN: 978-1-4759-6311-3 (sc)
ISBN: 978-1-4759-6312-0 (hc)
ISBN: 978-1-4759-6313-7 (e)

Library of Congress Control Number: 2012921987

Printed in the United States of America

iUniverse rev. date: 1/10/2013

Dedicated in Memory of

ELAINE T. SHUBECK

Special thanks you to:
My Family and Special Friends who helped
with words of wisdom and support.

Contents

Introduction

My 80+ years did present me with many opportunities not only to live life but to just watch it go by, and in some cases to write my observations. I hope my curiosity gave some insights that I will use to tickle your fancy and have you saying, "Yes. I never thought of that, but now I see."

While recuperating from a heart attack in 2004, I walked the streets of Cranford, New Jersey, and as a resident photographer, I recorded it's lifegiving beauty and atmosphere.

Since my wife died in 2007, and after a period of mourning, I have been writing to an old friend. No, "old" is not the appropriate word.

She is my long-time friend. (Over 60 years). I will say some of the writings do contain references to our present relationship. Marriage is not in our plans but after our friendship of over 60 years, (minus the years we were each married to someone else) we qualify as good friends.

During that time, I wrote in college and I free lanced writing for an advertising agency, though not seriously. I rewrote some old short stories for this book and updated them into the 21st Century. I tried to put a little mystery into the stories and present them as fun, informative and uplifting without sermonizing.

I particularly like my short story, "The Mystery of Cabin 828." In the same light, many thought "A Woman In Love," got inside them, as did, "What Makes a Man: a Man." "First Bacon," has a pleasant surprise as does "13D: Willie's Favorite Seat." I call them short stories but they are really short-short stories.

I smile every time I read, "Aged Out." But please don't linger on, "Love and Marriage." It's original title was, "Natural Conflict." You will probably find, "A Bachelor's Lament" is much more fun to read.

I suggest you limit yourself to only one story a night if you can in the "Potpourri," section. If you have any seniors around I also suggest a tissue-in-hand before you start to read, "Today I Saw a Friend." Then hurry to, "A He Named, a She," to give yourself a little lift.

O*bservations — Chapter 1*

Required Scribe

A writer I must be. Nothing else will satisfy me.
There are no fish in the sea that are attractive to me.
There is no game that I want to play.
Nothing can draw me off my keyboard and my paper, I say.

Even if it is a short story I seek within my brain,
I know I will try and try again to set it down and set it free.
I will go to you and in a flash I will present a lilting refrain.
See, I must write, and I must write whether it is good or just vanity.

There is nothing I can do. My head keeps telling my fingers to write.
They have no story to tell. Nor do they have a poem to sell.
They can only be a slave to the "story" tonight.
The story is within my head, and my job is to get it out.

I have no choice. I am a slave, as are my hands.
We just wait and then I am "told" what to expand.
And when I am done, I pick up the paper and read the verse
That I have written as the robot that I have become.

What has happened, and when did it start?
This is a mystery to me as well as to you.
But there comes a time, whether early or late,
When I must write upon the slate.

Poet Enclosed

If I have a poet inside of me, would I be telling you a lie?
I cannot call the sky red, nor can I call it blue.
I must be honest with you.
I don't know what to call it, oh my.

Could it be there really is a poet in me?
How can I find him and let him out?
How does one experience the glee
Of being able to say, "I have a poet in me"?

Yes, I know I must write and write as if my life is at stake.
I must write today and tomorrow and the day after that.
There is no shortcut, not a magic potion that I can take.
The only way to find a poet in me is to write and write to set him free.

Future Residence

My white rocking chair waits for me
In the gleaming morning sun and muted evening shadows.
It stands there in silent confidence that we will meet some tomorrow.
We are predestined to develop a special bond.

Yes, my white rocking chair waits for me.
It waits at the home with three others in a row.
It waits in pristine confidence just for me.
There seems to be one waiting for everyone I know.

White rocking chairs

I hope it will wait a very long time ...
And maybe even find another senior to support and rock.
I am in no hurry to give up and enter its waiting arms.
There is love and a life that I need to live.

There are mountains to climb and trips to take.
There are laughing friends still waiting for me.
Even meetings that I need to make.
There are morning dew and sunsets that I want to see.

I am not ready to sit in a white rocking chair.
But somehow I think it is not entirely up to me.
Somehow I realize, though I have never been on this road,
That there are plans afoot that include my meeting the white rocking
    chair.

Even though I am positive there is much that I still can share
Without sitting in that waiting white chair.
Whether it is on the dock with the gulls by the sea,
Or down the road with another group of three.

The trick you know is to get there when it is best for me.
I must get there while I am still awake and need not be restrained.
Even now I see some frailty sneaking up on me.
Must I leave some living and loving still undone?

5

There is a life's treasure of wisdom I have to share.
So maybe it is better to find a chair that is ready right now.
Even though we cannot see that it is really fair.
In the end, we will someday rock together somehow.

I'm Inside Out

I have my children and grandchildren watching over me.
I take care of myself pretty good. I wash my own clothes or take them to
    the cleaners.
I shower and I shave and I pay my own bills,
I take care of my own car, which I still drive.

I hang a little with the guys over coffee in the morning.
I still like women, and I think the female body is a thing of beauty.
I still challenge the devil for control of my soul.
I love my church, but I question some things, although I still serve it.

I cook and shop and sometimes clean the house. (Sometimes.)
I try to be a good father figure for my children and grandchildren.
I take pictures (some pretty). I write frequently (some good).
I try to remember old friends. Though widowers such as me are not too
    welcome among the married.

I try to be a good neighbor by being helpful.
I get away once in a while.
I manage and take my own medications.
I will even keep my mouth shut at times, though I like to rattle the cage
    occasionally.

I try to champion what is "right," at least what I think is "right."
I do not run as fast as in the past, nor jump as high, but neither does
    anyone else who I know.
I have some medical problems, but I still have enough energy to look to a
    future with a special friend.
I try not to be a burden to anyone.

Intentions Are Just ... Intentions

Today I will start my day full of energy.
I will conquer the world, at least my part of it, today.
I'll clean up the house and pick up all things gone astray.
I'll prove to myself that I keep a clean house, I say.

But I must get my breakfast and fill my belly.
I need the food to fuel my great plans for today.
There are first yesterday's papers in the living room to put away.
Actually, first I must clean the dishes out of the sink.

Now I can do the papers and get started in earnest.
But wait! Here is a story on the front page I have not read.
I'll stop now and read the story instead.
Oh, this story I must share with a friend. It is about a man loving
  a woman.

There, I have started, but it is a quarter to ten.
Where did the hours go? And I have not reached the end.
I also found a sports story that needs my attention.
This should take only a minute or two, I said ... now it is a quarter to
  two.

Lunch has passed me by—but I will take a break now and refill my
  stomach.
Can't work if my stomach is nagging to put something in it.
It can't take much more than a quick little minute.
I will have some yogurt and a rice cake with peanut butter on it.

My scale said I have gained four pounds in a week.
I will go on a very strict diet ... tomorrow ... I need all my energy for
  today.
There is much to do, and I must get started.
I will put the television on to keep me company as I work.

Oh, there is a ball game on today.
There's nothing better than that for a fan like me.
I'll take a moment and watch an at bat.
Oh, they are scoring. I'll see if the other team matches that.

Today I must cook supper; my son will be on his way.
Darn, I must run to the market. I am out of pasta right now.
I should plan for the month and cook only on Sunday
Then it would be easier to get my work done the rest of the week.

Well, supper is done, and now the dishes are in the sink.
I'll sit a moment and check the news.
Shucks, I fell asleep, and it is 10:30, I see.
I am alone, and I must take some time for a phone call.

It was so much fun talking on the telephone to my friend.
I don't see her often, but that will soon come to an end.
I must be careful and not mix today's papers with the others of the week.
I am happy that some are on a reader, and there are no papers to clean.

Well, time for bed. I will sleep and build my body for a trip.
I am not as young as I used to be.
A few hours on a plane can sap my energy.
But we will meet in the airport, and I will be in ecstasy.

And when I get back to my home, I will take time and straighten up.
I'll do the dishes, pick up the papers, and clean up the mess.
One can never tell who will be ringing my bell.
Even a bachelor cannot let everything go to hell.

Is This as Good as I Get?

Every time we look at the world, we see those who have success.
We also see those who seem to have much less.

What separates the successful from the rest?
Why do some always seem to do the best?

Yes, we could talk about intelligence, opportunities, or education.
We could even say that someone has a special situation.

But the truth is they are in the minority, and a very small one at that.
Most have prepared themselves to fulfill the dream they have placed
    under their hat.

But business and finance are only part of what we are.
We could say that personality is more important, by far.

For every little way that we succeed,
We can find failures—yes indeed.

But for every failure that we personally have, we can strive to turn it
    around.
We are alive and can change what needs to be changed if only it is
    found.

Some things can be changed in a day or two.
Some things might take a decade for me or for you.

But what makes us human is that we think we can change every
    outcome.
But what makes us human are our frailties, which we must first
    overcome.

We only think we see the future and think we can predict its path.
But only fools like me really think we can change its plans.

Aged Out?

I have just realized that I am becoming a senior member of the "aged out" club.

I have always been a member from day one, but now I have suddenly realized how many of the aged-out categories I belong in and that I never even realized existed. I could easily start with my infancy and list the crib, the bottle, the diapers (to which I may return someday), the sleeping interruptions (to which I have already returned), and the cooked-for person (which I hope to return to someday). But these are all natural progressions of any life.

What about some other things that are natural but hold so much pleasure I do not want to age out of them? For example, I am sorry that I aged out of playing in the sandbox, pulling pigtails, kissing, running, telling little white lies, and picking daisies for my mom.

I have even aged out of taking exams during May, hunting for a job (first and last), skinny-dipping in Newark Bay, and playing spin the bottle. Not to mention necking in the backseat (or front seat) of a car, smoking in the garage, and checking the wineglasses the morning after my parents' parties for whatever wine is left. Even asking a girl for a date, for a dance, or to take her home.

Of course, there are some things that I am happy to add to the aged-out list. I am elated to have aged out of reentering the army and waiting for the orders I might get. I am happy to have aged out of writing a college paper, sweating out final grades, choosing next semester classes, and meeting my new roomie ... and later meeting my special girl and waiting for the answer after I popped the question. Not to mention meeting her family—especially her father.

I have aged out of, or lived through, childbirth, parenting, graduations, new grandchildren, and divorces, along with various other family-related experiences such as illness and losing a spouse.

Now, of course, I very rarely age out of anything. I am much more likely to "age into" something. I must face aging into retirement with its lower income, more free time, restricted mobility, and any and all of the illnesses that go with old age—many of which I cannot pronounce or spell, but I have them.

I have already reached the age when I am being watched constantly to see if I have aged out of driving my own car, writing my own checks, taking my own medications, cooking for myself, or finding a date on my own ... or even writing a little observation such as this.

My Heart and I

I want to hear my heart go thump. It is important to me that it continues
 to pump.
Once my heart did stop on me. I thought that was all that I would be.
Then the doctors went inside to see if they could use their magic cutlery.
They took from here and put it there. They had many tubes sticking out
 of everywhere.
They shut down my heart, and I still lived. But I remember nothing and
 survived.
They acted like plumbers and cleaned my pipes.

When they started the pump again, I had to walk the floors.
My heart went too fast, and again I thought I had seen my last.
This time they stayed outside, and instead a pacemaker went inside.
It tells my heart when to pump and not to pump, so I can feel the
 calming thump.
Now all is going right, and I no longer feel the fright.
But a funny thing I learned the hard way that day ... I am not really here
 to stay.

A Little Smile

We have all received and given a little smile.
Do we realize what a wonderful gift that can be?
Are we not happy when we can say,
"That smile was directed at me"?
Does it not change your very day?
A smile is very small but very meaningful to us all.
It makes us instant buddies and sometimes even makes amends.
It soothes our hearts and helps us make new friends.
It helps us to feel secure that we are safe from every fall.
Now we are not talking about a little smile from a boy or girl.
And we are not talking about a smile that is "all knowing."
And certainly not the kind a teacher can give that lets us know we have
    been caught.
Or even a disapproving smile from a special date when we have been too
    late.
We mean a smile that soothes our heart and tells us we are welcome.
We mean a smile when we have made a gaff that tells us we can laugh.
We even mean a smile that promises us there is more to come.
When we thought the evening would have been "ho hum."
But there is another side to the story.
We have learned that it is more blessed to give than to receive.
So why not give a smile and light up your friends.
See the new sparkle in their eyes when they see a smile coming from
    you.
It really costs you very little and means so much to those you meet.
So as they say, "Give a smile and get a smile."
And you will be very surprised how even giving a tiny smile,
And then getting a smile, can help to make even your day.

Intelligent Life Survives

It is really true that one moment of being lax
Can change your life and exact a heavy tax.

One minute of not paying attention might bring you great pain
That could last a lifetime and drain whatever you gain.

You know not to speed and how to pick your friends.
You know where good starts and where good usually ends.

You know to use your brain and make right choices.
You know to choose and not listen to all voices.

You know to stick by your guns and not be dissuaded.
You know that talk is cheap, so don't be persuaded.

It is much better to be called chicken and stay alive
Than to give in to all and not survive.

Many times the choice is clear, and you cannot lose.
But there are times you must think for yourself before you choose.

By now you know that all is not so serious.
You have also learned that evil is not so mysterious.

If it is too good to be true then good it is probably not.
If it is too easy ... it is probably sleazy or hot.

Use the skills that are best for only you.
Use your knowledge of what you should do.

Be a good friend to friends who are yours.
Help each other in fighting all wars.

Life on the Seesaw

At any moment, any decision we make can be the difference between life or death. Believe it or not, we live on the edge. Of course, we realize we live or die in many different ways every day (physically, emotionally, financially, spiritually, ethically, and sexually—to name a few). Life and death surround us, and we are constantly choosing one and ignoring the other. Unfortunately, we are required to make choices both consciously and subconsciously, at times with a great deal of reflection and at times instinctively and instantly.

Physically: Let us consider for a moment the number of times today we have already made a decision that could have resulted in our injury or death, but we chose the correct path and have survived. Just leaving our driveway, getting out of the car, or crossing the street could have gotten us killed or gravely injured. In an instant, we could have become a paraplegic.

Emotionally: A poor choice of words or an emotional outburst could have destroyed a wonderful husband–wife or mother–daughter relationship. We could have done enough damage in a minute to cause us or our loved one years of emotional stress.

Financially: At the mall last night, we could have overspent on an evening gown or an unnecessary electronic gadget that we would be paying off for the next few years and using money better spent in another way.

Spiritually: How close are we to being tempted to do wrong? All things and relationships are fair game, you know. The greatest of these is doubt of the spiritual truths we have adopted and by which we live. We must constantly pray to repair our unbelief.

Ethically: We make subconscious choices concerning ethics. We do this so often that we do not even realize we are doing it. We walk a fine line daily, and one misstep could ruin us financially and emotionally. It could even result in punishment or jail.

Sexually: A lifetime of right decisions could be wiped out with one emotional misstep that results in the total collapse of our personal, family, financial, social, economic, and ethical lives. We are flirting with a form of living death as the result of a few moments of indiscretion brought on by passion or alcohol.

We are lucky to be alive. We are fortunate that our growth and training to be an adult has been so complete that we can live happy, productive lives without constantly needing to stop and evaluate our every move. But our vigilance must be constant and correct. Any failure can be death of some sort or at least years of tears and repair for the future.

We must be aware of the challenges we face. There is constant danger to our life and well-being. In this really hostile world, one misstep, one moment assuming things are okay, could result in disaster. This is especially true when we evaluate strangers. It is quite possible to misread a face or gesture to be nonthreatening when it is false, and we could be wrong about the potential danger. Not only does liberty require constant vigilance, life itself requires even greater vigilance.

Out of necessity, we are taught from early childhood to trust people. Realistically, the adult world is different from the world of our protected childhood. We are too good, too trusting, too naive to fully identify and defend ourselves without some reminders to be careful.

When you were a child, there was usually an adult to take on the responsibility of evaluating risks and being aware of your surroundings. Think what you would do in any threatening situation, and if you defend yourself, do so with all your energy, purposefully, and with complete abandonment. You must be willing to hurt and stop your opponent. Could you really do that as a ten- or twelve-year-old? Can you even do that now as an adult?

Performing the Laudable

What a world we live in! What are we becoming?

Every day I see more and more of a society that has lost its way. Our love affair for a reward for everything we do has morphed us into a do-nothing society.

We allowed someone else not only to decide what is right for us but to bend us to that action by playing games of denial or reward.

What has happened to our wonderful past, when we would do something because it was right—period. No ice cream. No lollipop. No gold star. No immediate or future reward.

Have we taken away the wonderful feeling of doing what is right because it is intrinsically right? We have sullied what is good and pure by placing a reward on it. Should I do what is "right" because I have either learned what is right or have come to my own conclusion as to what is right and then have the strength of character to do what is right for that reason alone?

How can we expect politicians to do what is right, even if there is no reward for them, when we cannot do that ourselves? How can we expect them to take the less popular paths and lead us in our more difficult responsibilities if we cannot do it ourselves? Considering our actions, how can we expect politicians to do what is right?

Uncooperative Behavior

Now there is a word that has gone from a word that can describe the good and bad to one that describes only the bad.

"Attitude" now means that a person is difficult to work with, one who is combative and will not listen to reason. In the past, it could easily mean the opposite and describe a person who was easy to work with and had a pleasant demeanor.

It really is a good word for us to work with today. It is one that helps us respond to self-talk.

Knowing its negative connotation, we can explore its more pleasant other side. Fortunately for us, because we have two hemispheres to our brain that communicate with each other, we can use this "split personality" to our advantage.

It is a common occurrence in life to have certain things bug us. They are just little things that recur and put us in a bad mood (attitude) immediately. But what if we recognize one of the negative things is about to happen to us, and instead of just letting it happen, we self-talk ourselves into seeing it as a fun thing, an inconsequential happening, or even an opportunity to do a good turn for someone else?

What a wonderful change we would have made in our attitude. How much more pleasant life can be if we eliminate even half of the things that bug us. All because we recognized a little problem, found a solution, and then, in just a minute or two, we changed the whole situation from anger to joy. We put a smile on our face, and because of that, we have improved the day of everyone we meet.

We can improve many things with a little self-talk, especially our attitude.

My Lap Waits

Beautiful woman, come sit upon my knee.
I promise no hanky-panky today.
I promise no fooling around, you see.
I promise just a little closeness and intimacy.

I would surely revel in that delight.
No, you say, you will not sit on my knee.
Even now, after all these years, and try as I might,
I cannot get you to sit on my knee.

I never thought of my knee as being too close.
But you know my knee better than me.
I know you know how I think and how I would choose.
Yes, it is better for you that you not sit upon my knee.

But I am John, and John is not usually put aside.
I will be asking you again for two or three years.
I will not try to sneak a little display.
So for sure you would not sit on my knee.

Sitting upon my knee has a certain intimacy for you and for me.
Unless there is an invitation somehow from you,
You are right if you say you will never sit upon my knee.
I must wait and wait for a sign that may never come.

Well, my friend, we have met again.
And the miles have not changed—and my heart is in pain.
The sun will not shine, and probably it will rain.
But within my heart you will always remain.

Helmets on Every Head

Do you think that just because you are an adult, you do not need a
    bicycle helmet?
Unfortunately, my friend, the rules of physics apply to young and old
    alike.
Whether you are a child or an adult, you are at risk.
It is really not just a scrape upon your knee that worries me.

You are thoughtful and duty bound to protect your girls or boys
From the ravages of permanent injury, such as a quadriplegia.
You do not want them to spend their life in a hospital bed.
Or do you think their life would be any better if you were there instead?

It is good and laudable for you to put a helmet on your child.
But a concussion is a concussion for young or old.
It is not the age but the distance from the top of the fall to the sidewalk
that causes the injury.
A taller adult has a greater distance to fall and, thus, is more likely to
sustain a greater injury.

Picture your children and what their life would be like if you sustained a
concussion.
Does your insurance take care of you for twenty years?
Can your children look at you lying there, still and dependent, without
any tears?
Is not the injury your common enemy instead?

So wear a helmet when you bike. Be a good example.
Protect your family from the injury ... either yours or theirs.
You are giving them a future by protecting both your heads.
You want them to be happy and live their life and not be a nurse to you
instead.

Unfair Vitality

It takes some time to learn about life.
It takes a decade or two and a great deal of strife.

It takes many wins and a couple of losses.
And it takes a special friend or two and a file full of bosses.

One must learn the hard way that fairness and honesty
Are ideals that are practiced in life and are not a curiosity.

You must learn that disappointments will come your way,
About that you have very little to say.

How you react to good or to bad
Is determined by you and maybe what education you have had.

Decisions in all things big or small,
Will determine your future and decide if you fall.

You must learn it is easier for things to go astray,
Than for things to go the other way.

You must learn as quickly as you can,
To find the good in each and every plan.

Remember what you do at any moment could last the rest of your life.
It could hurt you and maim you as sure as a knife.

You know to use your brain and make right choices.
You know how to choose and not listen to all voices.

You know not to speed and how to pick your friends.
You know where good starts and where good usually ends.

By the time you retire you will probably see
Two or three moments that really define your history.

It is never too early or too late to think about whether you will win or
    lose.
It comes faster than you think and reflects what you choose.

Your choices in your every decision are what your future is really made of.
So build your future with intelligence, goodness, and love.

Ultimately Benefit?

It has been said that in the long run we will not do anything that is not
    to our own benefit.

Can I find an answer to the question of how to do good for someone
    else?

Am I able to find something within myself to give me an understanding as to my behavior?

Can everything I do be reduced to its most basic value, and there it will be found to be only in my best interest?

Is my loving someone of interest only to me, because, ultimately, it makes me feel good?

My giving a gift is an example of "It is more blessed [to me] to give than to receive," and is that why I do it?

Can I even think of one thing I do for anyone else that will not ultimately be of benefit to me?

Is everything I do, or attempt to do, just an exercise to satisfy my ego or some other need that is beneficial to me?

Is all my talk about loving someone and wanting to do things for them just an attempt by me to satisfy some need within myself?

Do I truly believe that helping you, even in some very small way, will benefit only you and in no way benefit me?

And if I find that I am the ultimate beneficiary of all that I do or not do, how can I ever do anything just for you?

Loneliness and Despair

Yes, my dear, what are we to do?
There is little—or nothing—we can do.

It is all out of our hands.
It is all in his hands and his heart.

Oh yes, we can play it cool and do nothing ... and just wait.
I cannot say why we wait or what we wait for.

But let me tell you that is not what I want to do.
If I make a mistake, I possibly may live my life in lonely despair.

If I do nothing, I will surely live my life in loneliness and despair.

A*mour — Chapter 2*

A Woman in Love

What a folly this could be! A man—an older man such as me—to be talking about a woman in love. Who else but a man who has loved women all his life—single, cruising, courting, married, or widowed like me? Of course, I have not experienced all things. Nor do I want to experience them all. But a woman in love is loved by everyone, and if that love is directed at you or me, we will truly have heaven here on earth.

Love Bouquet

What is it about a woman in love that gets our attention? Is it the joy within her eyes? Is it the spring in her step? Is it that wonderful panache that radiates when she enters a room? Could it be that certain aura she exudes that really stirs our heart? We will not notice the rain or the snow, because we feel so good.

She will make you alive, and you will want to be at her side. Her joy and exuberance light up your world. She is as vital as she will ever be. She is a joy for you and a joy for all those all around. Her laugh is contagious. Her smile weakens every knee.

If it happens to you, and I pray that it does, you will forget the world is falling apart. The sun will shine, the breezes will be cool, and the birds will sing a joyful melody.

You want her to talk to you and ask a favor—while you hope she will not, because you are not so sure you will answer her coherently. And as for the favor she might ask, you will promise anything and then figure out how to do it later.

Her clothes will fit every curve of her body, whether in your imagination or in reality. Maybe it is because she is standing straight, and her body is alive with anticipation. Let's face it, she is presenting herself to her lover and happily so.

But best of all is for it to be the woman sitting across the breakfast table from you. Your friend, your mate, your reason for being. As time goes by, you will both find the troubles of the world will certainly wear you both down. But it only takes a smile from either to bring back that special ecstasy.

Just take a moment now and make her feel like a woman. You will see she will make you feel like a man. She will be that woman in love— joyful, playful, and tender to you. When you are together, she will quicken your pulse and stir your insides. It matters not what is happening to the rest of the world.

Improbable Things

There are impossible things happening in my life.
Well, if not impossible, at least highly improbable.
Every man hopes to meet one great woman.
No man would expect to meet two great women in all this strife.

I certainly felt blessed and honored to have met and married my wife.
God proved himself to be a loving God with that match, you see.
He also proved how incomplete I was by sending such a great helpmate.
After she died, he sent me another special friend.

Yes, two beautiful women in the life of one man.
That is really pie in the sky.
But as you know, he knows what to do.
Not me, not me—I would never think of two.

Of course, as humans we really don't understand.
Is it impossible or just highly improbable?
Well, not live together actually, just friendship, you see.
My dear friend that is what is happening to me.

I could tell you this story until I am blue.
I could give you details, but you will not change.
Though I am wonderfully spry for a senior my age,
I would at least be your companion for the rest of your life.

I tell you don't think why, don't think how.
Just grab hold of my coat,
And pull me close and kiss me right now.
For I am older, and the question could soon be moot.

Together we should be. Yes, that is what I said.
What more do you want while I still have my breath?
We are too soon old and sometimes too soon dead.
But now we are alive, and I am chasing after you.

Here is what you can do when I catch up to you.
Just present your lips, and step into my arms.
Grab hold of me while I am close to you.
Pull me closer, and I will love you and promise no harm.

This Is Your Day

The light of the sun has chased the gloom of night.
It has warmed the air, spread the fog, and is greeting a new day.
A bird is praising the dawn and calling his mate to see if she is near.
A sentinel scans the sky and proclaims to those around, "All clear."

A chipmunk runs across the grass and scurries beneath a bush.
A red-tailed hawk circles above his field, seeking his morning fare.
Two mourning doves, sitting side by side, are singing their little duet.
The wise old fox has settled in his den for the day.

Your alarm stirs you from your dream-filled sleep.
And as you step into the world, you feel the floor beneath your feet.
A sip of fresh coffee to chase the cobwebs from your mind.
Yes, it feels good to finally feel alive.

You kiss your wife, and she chases you ... with a chuckle.
But leans over and whispers in your ear.
Yesterday has past ... tomorrow is yet to come.
But for you ... this will be a great day.

Cupid's Day

Some would say, "St. Valentine's Day gladly comes but once a year."
Why would one say that of such an opportunity is not clear?
A chance to tell your love that you love her dear.
A chance for a sweet kiss and a whisper in her ear.

A chance to share the beauty and joys of life with your girlfriend or your
    wife.
A chance for a kiss upon your cheek, even in the middle of the week.

A scrumptious meal with no dishes to clean.
A comforting shoulder on which to lean.
A soft hand to hold ... by heck.
A tender arm around your neck.

Bringing you closer to love-sweetened lips.
Maybe even a hand upon her hip.
But more than all this friendly stuff, you will hear many things about
    yourself.

She will tell you how nice you are.
How thoughtful of you to bring a candy bar.
Your choice of flowers she will enjoy.
As well as the card and whisper, "Oh boy."

It gives you the words that you want to say.
But writing rhymes is not your play.
So better that you say it through the card.
The price is fair, and the writing too hard.

Of course, there is always the dilemma of wanting to say more but not
    scare her away.
Or wanting to say less without distress.
Say everything just right, and you might caress.

For it is coming just once a year.
The love you express on St. Valentine's Day is in your heart the whole
    year round.
So tell her every day, and your true love will respond.

Love Shines in Me

You are rushed today, but I just want to say, "You are a series of wonderful thoughts." I always marvel how we can talk, and you seem so happy with me. My little problem is I see you as a wonderful, brilliant, and beautiful gem, and I worry you will suddenly wake up and realize I am just an average bloke and not worthy of all your special attention.

I have little to offer you. Maybe a little smile and a soft embrace. Some memories, both good and bad. Many questions and some poetry to make you laugh. You have a car. You have a house. You actually have me, but that's the point. I try to be a nice guy. I try to be whatever you want or need. I try to be supportive and understanding. I certainly try to be near you. My feelings for you mean a great deal to me as do your feelings for me.

Only you know how helpful you are to me. You are a calming voice. A beautiful, mature, and loving woman I can embrace. You are mysterious. Sometimes I wonder how you see me. How can I fit into your life? How can I answer your needs, those you now have and those that are yet to be? I try to lighten your day, but I probably only make more work for you along the way.

Let it be whatever it is. There is only a tiny part of you that needs someone who cares. A part that sees a little emptiness in your life. Let me be that answer for you. I have lived a long life—or so they say. I have learned a little along the way—or so I say.

I see happiness and joy in our being together, and I see loneliness and sorrow when we are apart. If I could, I would come to you when you feel overwhelmed by the things around you and at least give you a soft tissue. I would hold your hand when you were confronted by steps. I would get the Sports Creme in the middle of the night. I would check outside when it was dark to chase the demons away. I would get the things you needed to put on your plate. And I promise I would help you clean up the kitchen after we ate. I would even get you a pot or a pan, so you could make your wonderful spread. I certainly do not want you to become dependent on me. I just want to lighten your load and give you some time to get off your feet and sit close to me.

Not much to offer, I will admit. But offered with love. We never know what is ahead of us or what we will need. It is one thing to be alone and as spirited as you are, and be able to take care of yourself. But it is another thing entirely when you need a friend, someone who cares about you, someone who feels every pain you have with empathy and love. Someone to tell you that you are loved and are special to him—me.

Well, this is a bit longer than I had expected, but I have this light in my eyes that moves me close to you. If you think you can go it alone, then I am helpless. I think it would be better for us to be together somehow.

Life Is about Love

We seem to either take life for granted or don't live it when we can. Do we ever look at the sun and marvel at its existence? Do we ever think it is marvelous that we can look at the sun? Are the warm, life-giving rays being cursed for shining in our eyes? Would we do better than that if we were in control? Would we have invented the hat or some kind of clouded glasses to allow us to see the wonders of the world beneath our feet? Would we have noticed the worm under the grass—a robin's breakfast—or an ant marching in line to an invisible drummer's beat?

What have we done in thanks for being alive? Have we helped another creature, large or small? Have we relieved another human's stabbing pain? Or even spread some love upon our mate in thanks for thinking only the best of what we do. How about a tender reward for her loving me, even though I constantly ignore her plight while she takes care of me. Even I could think of a hundred things I could do to give her a smile.

Yes, we have opportunities to bring love to others. But this is not about others; it is about us and our love. It's about you and me being aware of the rest of the world and taking a stand with a helping hand. It's about not looking the other way when we have a choice to make. It's not only about loving those who love us but loving those who have not discovered that life is all about love.

You and I are the only creatures on earth who are not food for another creature. Think of it, my friend, we are the top of the chain. What have we done to warrant that position?

Love and Marriage

It seems to me that Western civilization has love and sex confused. In many cases, they are diametrically opposed to each other, and yet, they are intimately connected. Other than in Shakespeare, how often does the reality of mother and son having sex occur? To most in our culture, it is not even something to joke about.

But how often is there sex in a marriage where there is no love? Much too often, I presume. Many couples profess love, but abuse that love and use and abuse sex on a regular basis. It is used as a tool to get what one wants. It is used as a tool to exert dominance over another person. It is used to satiate our own desires. But who am I to say what is right or wrong? Who am I to say it is used or abused? That is not up to me.

It is much more difficult to exhibit love and concern for another person day in and day out than to jump into bed for a few minutes and then get on with other things. Loving someone, truly loving someone, commits one to a lifetime of giving and supporting. The wonder of wonders is when two people truly love each other. That is when love creates a special, wonderful life. In most marriages it does occur, but only sporadically. Unfortunately, each individual's ego gets in the way of a true commitment.

Also making the state very difficult to achieve is that our society treats love and commitment as almost impossible to attain, and if it does not occur spontaneously, it does not occur at all. But reality requires that love and commitment be the ultimate goal in most marriages, so there is a commitment by both to the dedication of emotions, time, effort, and assets to reach that goal. There are no shortcuts; it is a long-term effort. At times, a lifelong commitment is required to achieve meaningful unity. It takes many, many decisions of self-denial and loving actions, with little or no immediate benefits, for the couple to achieve this unity.

The idea the couple must be fully dedicated to each other seems to be in opposition to common sense, but the result is not confusion or a stalemate. It is a state of euphoria that translates into a wonderful life. The goal of love with service results in life becoming a wonderfully long journey of foreplay and joy. All actions bring the couple closer together. The resulting union is one of ultimate surrender and unity, and with care, it can be achieved over and over again. The change from honeymoon to everyday life is not the leaving of the honeymoon suite but the change of focus by the individuals from self interests to caring and sharing.

It is to everyone's benefit to make this transformation and remain in this wonderful state. We must understand the concept of giving and apply it freely to our special relationship in the joyful commitment of loving service. That desire to give is within us all, but so is the desire to take and use other people. With care and dedication, we can choose the giving of loving service. Repeated a hundred times a day, it will become easier and easier to make that choice. And without noticing it, we will slip into a life of togetherness and support.

Present Love

Let me chase you in the snow.
Let us be like kids again.
Let us laugh and play together.
Let me kiss your cold, wet cheek to prove I am no longer meek.

Let us play and get some snow upon my face.
I'll hold you close and then we can really trace
The years and tears and ploys of life.
The life that seemed to end in strife.

Young life is gone, as are our lovers, you say.
But we are left to find a new way.
To live on with some bits of joy and love.
Of togetherness for you and for me.

Our job now is to pick up the pieces
And to make sense of loneliness and folly.
To try to figure out why some things happen,
Will only lead to our being jolly.

You have found the answer to the riddle.
There is no answer is what you say.
We just pick up the pieces and try to be merry,
While life goes on, and we can go along each day.

We do the best we can and wonder
If the path we choose now is the best for us.
There are no rockets, no whistles to sound.
Just peace and friendship are what we have found.

The joy of someone who cares about me,
Who watches the clock when I am late,
Who tells me to be careful on the ice,
Who holds her hand out to be nice.

What more could I want? What more do I need,
But someone for me to love and someone to love me back?
Someone who cares and gives the house its life.
Who warms me with a smile and the touch of her hand.

Love Must Grow to Live

I am sure you have heard it said that one must grow in order to live.
A thought like that can bring you great dread.

When even to stand still will not suffice, you see,
For standing still is like kissing ice to me.

And you know it is true that every day we fail to move ahead
Is a day that we have lost some of our life instead.

There is nothing we can say or do to stop or change it.
Life is a journey ... like a trip upon the highway.

Change will come for you and me.
It could come slowly and with great stealth.

Or come like lightning and in our face.
Certainly when we least expect its cold embrace.

So it is a question for us to ponder right now.
We must decide and plan to move ahead somehow.

Our being together is most important to our life.
Nothing else will keep away the strife.

Be ready to help love grow, whether it is new or old.
Be ready every day, or someday you could be in the cold.

So even though you say we are special friends.
And it seems to me that true love must grow to live.
Now is the time for us to ponder what we will do.
When that special someone says to us, "I do love you."

Separated, Why?

Where have you been all these years?
Why can I not see you through my tears?
When will you say, "Good morning, John."
Or must I sit here and forever be alone.

Where is the good feeling inside when I hold your hand?
When can we laugh at something silly?
When can I smile at your beautiful face?
When will be our next embrace?

I pray our life together has not ended.
I pray our time apart is not extended.
How can the birds perform for you and for me,
If we do not stand at the window to see?

There goes the pair of goldfinches, searching for food.
There go the cardinals, feeding together.
There are the doves, cooing and cooing.
What the heck are we still doing?

It is obvious to me, and I hope to you,
That together for us is better by far.
Friendship and working side by side
Is how I want us to abide.

Well that may be true, but not today
Our togetherness is now on hold.
That is not to say I am happy this way,
But that is life, or so I am told.

Yes, my friend, this is reality in all its gory glory.
Our love, togetherness, and friendship must be put on hold.
"Patience" is our word of the day.
Waiting and loving is just our present way.

Just a Word about Us

As the years goes by, and I wonder why
We are such good friends, there are no ends.
It is unbelievable to me, and you can probably see.
I can still find a place, behind that beautiful face.

Could it be that the more we find, the more that we will bind.
We will be better friends, and I will want to hold you close to me.
Although even those smiles, cannot conquer the miles.
The question right now, will you want me to stay somehow.

Am I real or just a fake, and all I want is your heart to take.
That is not the case with me, it truly is the beauty that I see,
There is a glow within your heart, right from the very start.
Yes, I can see, what no other woman means to me.

Is it love, or friendship for my soul, or are they both in control?
The future I cannot comprehend, but I want it to never end.
I think that friendship is more difficult to do, because when I look at you,
You stir within my heart ... no, I do not want to start.

All I can say right now is, I want to be close, and I don't know how.
But in some special way, there will be a beautiful day.
And I will give you a peck, right on your neck.
That will lead to a jump and a sigh, and a clap and an, "Oh my."

We will go hand in hand, and we will stand
In front of every friend, and they will see that there is no end.
There is loving and caring, there is a profound sharing.
There is friendship forever, with an end that is never.

My Heart Sees You As ...

A sight for sore eyes.
A cool breeze on a hot day.
A sunny break in the clouds of a thunderstorm.
A spring shower to melt the winter ice.
A beautiful sunset after a tiring day.
The morning sun to chase the night.
Balm for my chapped lips.
An ottoman for my tired legs.
A soak for my sore feet.
A bed for my exhausted body.
A shoulder for a weary brain.
Music for my ringing ears.
Water for my parched lips.
Calm for my confused mind.
Companionship for my lonely heart.
Structure for my turmoil.
Friendship for my hostile world.
A warm body for my yearning arms.
Hope for my future.
A life where I felt no life.
Love for a tired heart.
A smile from a longtime friend.
A blessed answer to my fervent prayers.

S*pecial Poems — Chapter 3*

Little Bluebird

Little bluebird, why are you blue?
Are you like your mother or your dad?
You are so cute I want to cuddle you.
Why are you playing in my yard?

Little Bluebird

Do you hide in the trees or on the ground?
Are you so low I must get on my knees?
Or must I look in the sky for you to be found?
If I build a bird box, will you stay with me?

Come closer to me, and let me see.
What is inside of your pretty little eyes?
Do you see me as well as I see you?
And tell me, little friend, what do you eat?

Do you eat seeds all through the year?
Do you help to keep my garden free of bugs?
And call your mate before the morning sun comes up.
Will you dance for her and defend her from all intruders?

I know if you are a male, you do not build the nest.
But after the female builds it for your brood,
You will help to feed the clutch,
And you will defend her and the rest.

Bluebird, bluebird, I am glad you are near.
I will fix you a birdbath and build a house for you.
Stay in my yard, as you are welcome here.
I would love to see you come back year after year.

Life and Death on Display

There they are piled in the street and on the lawn.
The mountains of grief as far as one can see.
Yes, there they are, both sides of this street.
The hurricane came down this street, destroying it all.

Mountains of grief as far as one can see, Cranford, NJ.

A lifetime of hope set out in the sun.
There is your neighbor's dreams before your eyes.
Just waiting for a garbage truck to haul them away.
Thank God everyone survived that night of fright.

But you can see as well as me,
The floods did damage to hearts and to homes.
The water rose as high as a tree,
To destroy property and many a memory.

Then it did its dirty work of soaking everything it could find.
It ruined all kinds of furniture and appliances in its way.
And now it all sits outside in soggy decay.
Lining the street, these mountains of grief.

These are not just household items stretching to infinity.
These are dreams and joys and pictures and toys.
These are mementos, good and bad, all tattered and wet.
The mountains of grief are history spread before your eyes.

This is a record of the lives of both living and dead.
It is more than just things bought shiny and new.
It is things that have lived and now are battered and blue.
Everything here has a special story to tell.

There is a favorite chair and a lock of a child's hair.
There are feeding tables and cribs full of memories.
And desks and books and records and notes.
They all represent a little piece of someone's heart.

They are the lives of this little neighborhood.
Through snow and rain and summer heat.
The people have moved on to rise above defeat,
And so they again will conquer these mountains of grief.

Remain Reclined

I tried so hard to stay in bed.
I tried and tried not to lift my sleepy head.
But try as I might, and try I did,
I had to raise my sleepy head.
Some would say that is a silly thing.
The problem is not to stay in bed.
The problem is how to get up instead.
See the problem really is within my head.
I have not learned in all these years.
I must take command and be my boss.
I must take control of my mind.
I cannot let my wayward thoughts take control.
I should have learned by now that there are tricks
That I must play upon my brain.
I cannot let the physical me control my life.
I must strive to listen but still assert my will.
I must engage in a little self-talk.
No, not out loud in a public place,
But quietly within my private space.

My brain talks within itself so I, too, must get within the loop.
Then I will find that I will do what I want to do.
It will be the things that are important to me.
You will not see another time when I will say,
"I want to stay in bed today."
All I must do is take control.
I must be the boss of my body.
I must not let it do its will.
Then yes, oh yes, then I can stay in bed.

Rising Sun

Yes, I can see the sun rising far away.
I can feel the surge of energy within my soul.
I realize that I have been given a new day
To fight the fight and stay off the shoal.
There is nothing that is guaranteed, you know.

But it is a good start for us here below
To feel the sun's warmth and realize that we are on our way.
A wonderful proof that we have at least a part of this new day.
But what will we do with this glorious gift?
What will we do to warrant such a new chance?

Will we be able to heal a killing rift?
Will we make someone special happy?
Will we find a cure for any deadly cancers?
Will we solve the mysteries of the universe?
Will we become part of world-class scholars?

All are good and very diverse
But way beyond our circle of friends.
Our influence is limited to those around us.
But we are all still human and can always make amends
To those in need of a helping hand.

We now have another chance to help someone else.
We can use our strength and our humanness.
We can refuse to let our selfishness smother
Our urge to lift the burden of another.
We need not take the world by storm.

We need not make the mountains fall.
All we need is to make our love the norm.
And bring peace and harmony to our world.

There Are Lessons to Learn

Are the heavens shedding a soft rain today?
Or are the angels sending some tears our way?
Is our being apart breaking even their heart?
Are they feeling human today—because of our way?

If you feel that we are meant to be, then dear friend come and sit with
    me.
Don't they realize that humans rarely have a balance of joy and despair?
We must suffer the awful truth that we live in time.
We struggle now and wait for our blessings to start.

But as I look into my heart, I feel a certain sadness there.
It is you I must seek to improve our fate.
We know it is terrible that we have both lost a mate
But it is wonderful we have found each other.

There is no substitute for a loved one lost.
There is no way for the sadness to go away,
Except to live as best we can while the years go by.
And we learn to live with those that are here today.

It is the fate of all creatures that walk the earth
To live and love with sadness and with mirth.
It is hard to say that ... because we come ... and then we go.
But believe me when I say that we must journey so.

In every raindrop that falls by day
There is sadness mixed in with joy.
We must somehow learn to love anew.
But some of us never learn. Yes, sadly there are a few.

Your Dear Life

Yes, it is true, my friend, time does fly.
Certainly for mortals such as you and I.
We must reach out, grab on, and hold on for dear life.
Then we will fly with it to its wonderful heights.

Yes, not only life, but ... our dear life.
Not a life with a touch of the mundane and in which there is only a little
    comfort.
But a life that's full of life.
Where there is love, a special relationship, and lots of joy.

But when the sun does shine and the sky is a special blue.
When there are birds singing to each other and to me and to you.
When there are special, wonderful, enriching smells to stir our inner
    memories.
When we can really feel alive ... and not just be alive.

When all the world is right. Or at least the world that we are in.
When not having answers and not seeing our future is not a thought
    and brings dismay.
When we seem to tingle at a special touch and a special look.
When the focus of our life is just inches away ... we are truly alive.

That is when our God smiles upon us, and that is when we ... smile at
    him.
That is when life is really life as it is meant to be.
When every breath will bring happiness and joy.
When we have made our life a life of love.

But, of course, we all know that it is not only up to us.
We must reluctantly agree that not all of what we live
Is shaped by us or how we see what comes our way.
But whether we are happy or sad is mainly up to you and I.

Freedom Required

I need to be free. I need to be me.
I need my freedom ... just to be free is enough for me.
What matters if every side tells me what to be?
I need to be free to be just little old me.

Why can I not be me? Why must everyone take a side?
Let me be free if I want to go out or stay inside ... let me decide.
Why cannot everyone think like me?
Why must I get permission for my every move?

Why should anyone want to say to me, "It's snowing out"?
And then they say, "You cannot leave the house."
I can see it is snowing out. I have seen snow before.
I know what the doctor has done to me and what he has said.

I know he wants to fix me up to be with you for as long as I can.
But does he not see that I am a man, and the decision is up to me.
Or could it be that I have crossed the line some time ago.
Have I now gone backward with the years and cannot even see the
    snow?

What is the sense of seeing the beauty and then hearing, "Stay inside."
Who, me? I can see it is too slippery. In my condition I know I cannot go
  outside.
But please, my dears—yes with an s—all of you, I am still a man, and I
  can decide
If it is safe or not for me. I don't want to crack my head. I have decided
  to stay inside instead.

I know it was not easy to let me be me, but I guarantee I will continue to
  let you be you.
I will not change and say to you, "Stay inside," "Put on a hat," or, "Don't
  shovel the snow."
I will not change the lessons I have taught you these past fifty years.
I am proud of your adulthood; I will always want you to be free.

So let me be free ... until the time when I cannot choose.
Then I want you to say to me, "It is time, dear Dad, for me to say, 'Stay
  inside.'"
The difficulty, my dear, is there is no line in the sand to tell you when.
A day too soon will shatter my ego. A day too late might shatter my
  head.

But that is your job. My job was to help you grow and put you in school.
I would bandage the scrapes and soothe the tears.
I taught you to drive and hopefully stay alive.
Just so you can say, "Dad, there is ice out there. Please stay inside."

Did It Snow Again?

Do you have much snow this morning?
We have a new dusting to place us in mourning this morning.
It portends a beautiful, clean whiteness to look at today.
But by now, clean or dirty, they can take the blasted snow away.

45

But not you, my friend, I want you to stay and be by my side
To build a snowman when we are outside,
To shovel the walk and pick up the mail,
To change the bulbs and sweep the hail.

The path is long and treacherous, you see.
A journey of friendship for you and for me.
It is not lonely usually, but we have some loneliness to fight.
But together we can make the journey a delight.

There is much for you and for me to do together ...
In friendship and folly. For example, just laughing at the weather.
And though we can still function alone,
God made men and women to be compatible prone.

Our main job in the world, you will see,
Is to choose our works and set our priorities.
For with all there is to do, from small to large,
We need to clean up all the hodgepodge.

But people are most important, I insist.
And those we love should be at the top of the list.
But again, I say, you have your personal needs to meet.
From head to toe, from your nose to your feet.

You must think of you first ... you must take care of yourself.
Though beautiful as you are, there are no new parts upon a shelf.
Everyone else, be they family or even the pope,
Must take a backseat and live only in your hope.

Winter Snow

As you and I sleep in winter's cold,
Mother Nature has left us a present to behold.
Now I wonder if it is really a treat
To have so much snow under my feet.

Of course it is cold ... winter is cold by its nature.
You and I know that nature does not love or hate.
Nature does its thing on you and me
And says to us that is how it will be.

Take it or leave it. Like it or heave it.
It is not what you want that will be.
It is what Mother Nature wants that we shall see.
Call Mother Nature a witch, but spell it with a B.

Yes, you can laugh at me, but we both have cold feet,
A runny nose, frozen toes, and heating bills to meet.
We both wait and plead for spring flowers to see,
And Mother Nature says, "You shall see ... but when is really up to me."

If you can call this a little prose, then my talent I cannot hide.
My friends may moan, and my friends may groan.
They see no poetry in what I write.
But I just smile and leave their sight.

All Snow Must Go

Snow. Dear snow, it is time for you to go.
I have had enough of your depressing gray days.
Your dirt and grime have laid me low.
Dirty snow, all snow, will you please ... just go.

Once you were white as you know what.
But now you are messy and full of grime.
Even dogs are having difficulty finding a place
Where they have not already visited.

So why are you waiting? The sun to shine?
The rain to wash you away? Or a new snow that is fine
And covers you up and makes you white again?
Then you can stay, but beneath the new snow and hidden.

You had your day, and still you linger.
Can you not see that there is a zinger?
There is no way that you can stay.
The temperature is warming up, and you will soon melt away.

Dirty snow—clean or dirty snow—you have stayed too long.
You must leave; it is quickly understood.
But come next May, on that distant day,
I will be happy to say ... you will have gone away.

Be Careful at Sea

Be careful on the sea.
In a moment, it can turn on thee.
Mother Nature cares not about you or me.
You are a guest upon her sea.

Sometimes I think Mother Nature is a witch.
Sometimes I spell it with a B.
But be that as it may,
Sure as heck, she will turn on you some day.

From Santa to Me

Santa, Santa, I thought you did not visit me!
I peeked under the tree last night before I went to sleep.
And I gave myself an awful fright.
Try as I might, I saw nothing there from your flight.

How could you have missed me and passed me by?
I thought you checked me twice last year, and I would be okay.
I was really looking for my gift under the tree.
But I looked and looked, and I saw nothing.

I cried myself to sleep and into the terrible dreams.
But when I got up this morning and saw the tree,
You had been there; you had visited me ...
Boy ... next year no checking the tree before I go to sleep.

Life's Cruel Nature

Oh, sir, will you be my friend to the end?
How absurd to say, "to the end."
We must live today, for it will too soon go away,
And we will have had nothing, just the end.

So what about right now, with its love and joy?
I say, "Friend, live for now, and forget the end."
Grasp what we have while it is here before us.
Embrace it and encase it in your memory.

For soon the end will come
And we will be old and gray.
We will be feeble and only say,
"If this be the end, let it go away."

I am not ready to give up my "now."
I spent too much time looking for the end.
And now that the end is here, I want to say,
"Please go away, and give me another day."

How Will We Die?

Please answer me, my friend.
How would you like your life to end?

Psychologists seem to like to say
That we wonder about our very last day.

The older we get the more mindful it is to us.
We cannot forget that life will not be forever thus.

Like all things, good or bad, there are changes just ahead.
But some would hope for no changes instead.

But whether we want to or not.
To choose our death is not our lot.

We know not when or where death will come.
We know not how, in the end, we will succumb.

But life is more important for me, you see.
Just how do we live is of relevance to me.

It matters not how your life will end.
It matters how your life you did spend.

Very few of us are remembered for more than a little while.
We are remembered for how we lived and what was our style.

Our legacy will be our contribution to everyday life.
What was our donation for easing the strife?

Did others waste their time raising us with hardship and hard work
For us to die with little more than a big, wide smirk?

What have we left behind when we have come to our end?
That is the true test of our greatness in life, my friend.

Change of Heart

"We shall see, we shall see." That is what you say to me.
But we will only see it if we both live to be hundred and three.
I have never known a man who could pull off that trick,
Unless, of course, a man has, and he has kept it a secret.

Can you keep a very important secret about me?
I will at least make a subtle pass at you every day of my life.
I want to be the second to know if you change your mind.
I know you will be the first to know.

I almost said, "Changed your heart."
I realize that we can do very little changing of our hearts.
But if your heart does change, then you will change your mind.
And I will lean lean over and kiss your cheek.

By then, you may find that all I will be able to say is "Thank you."
But that is what I can do now.
So what is the big deal?
I guess it is again that male ego thing or the tiger in me.

But I know that you know, and that is how it will always be.
Unfortunately, you also know that my daily pass at you will not be too
    subtle.
It might be subtle to me but certainly not to you.
I don't think I have ever been subtle to you.

What Makes a Man ... a Man?

What a question, "What makes a man ... a man?"
Everyone seems to know the answer to just that.
You can tell him by his hat.
Plain and simple, take a look at his crown.

A Hat?

That's not the answer; it is much too easy.
There is more to being a man
Than what he puts upon his head.
What's inside; what's he made of, we must ask instead.

Is it strength; is it bulk?
Is it courage in time of danger?
Will he stand up to a bloke?
Will he stand there and take a poke?

Will he be a shepherd to his woman?
Will he hold her tenderly?
Will he make her special in his life
When he asks her to be his wife?

Will he nurture their children and help them adults to be?
Will he teach them by his example of strength and honesty?
Will he be gruff and tough, or will he be gentle and loving?
Could he be all these things and still be a man?

Will his gruffness be tempered by his kindness?
Is it possible to be a man and still show love?
Some would say that is a weakness and out of character.
But for you and me, love is the most important attribute to see.

All else about a man is out of focus. All else fails to do a thing.
All else just causes trouble and turmoil.
And if he has not love, he is doomed to be a failure.
Love is what makes a man ... a man.

Let no one fool you. Take anything else away and it's okay.
But take away love, and you have no man.
And by the way, you can use this definition
To tell the world, "Love is what makes a woman ... a woman."

Why Do We Not Live Today?

That is a question I ask myself almost every day. Is life so bad that we do not want to live it now? Do you ask it of yourself? Why do we want to give up "now" and hope for something better in the unknown future? What makes us think life will be any better at some future time?

Of course, we all have problems every day. Everybody and everything has problems every day. Even our breathing constantly is an attempt to solve the problem of getting enough oxygen to stay alive. We do it almost constantly and certainly without thought, until we need extra oxygen. Then we become aware of the need and immediately take corrective action by inhaling heavily or reducing our need by resting. If we must struggle for every breath, why would you think that anything else would be easier? To struggle is to live. To win the struggle is to be alive.

The challenges are here and now. Solve the challenges of today, and the future, with its own problems, will at least have successes to build upon. Usually problems, or challenges, only grow more difficult as they—or you—age. Nip your problems in the bud, when they are smaller than they will be some future day. You probably will not be much richer tomorrow. You certainly will not be younger. You might be a little wiser. But if you live in the future, you will have missed living today's challenges and joys.

Some will say, "Smell the flowers every day." And I agree. But I also say be alive and enjoy today.

A silly game. A fleeting hug. A goofy face. They are all rewards for your labors of today. They will never again grace your life in exactly the same way. Grab the love that is here right now. That is your reward or living the fight right now.

Who can say that your spouse will be there, or here, tomorrow? Who can say for sure that you will be here tomorrow or even tonight? Say thanks and give praise today. Tomorrow may be too late. "It" does not always happen to the other guy.

Let us see the good and reject the bad. Let us take every opportunity for joy and praise today, and leave the sorrow for tomorrow. Maybe, just maybe, if we have enough joy today there will be less sorrow tomorrow. If not, we will at least have lived today and have fewer regrets in the end.

A Friend

A gift every day—why we don't even get mail every day, and yet I say, "a gift every day." Think of something you receive or experience every day. What about food? Well, maybe, but I am thinking about something a little more substantial than food. Maybe even a little more helpful.

Well, my friend, you greet, meet, help, interact, and are helped by at least one friend every day. In the same proportion that you are helped, friends are a gift to you. The more help you get and give the more friends you have.

Think of all the ways you are helped. I venture to say that one might not get though the day without a friend's help.Whatever you need to survive, friends seem to have waiting for you.

They can answer your questions about the stock market. Well, they could in the past.
Do you need a ride? Do you want to hide? Do you need some money? Call a friend.
You have a broken heart. Now that's not funny ... but call a friend.

Even more important than answering your needs, what have you done to help your friend? A ride to the train or the plane? A bottle of milk while you shop for yourself.
A few bucks right now to carry them over. Or even an ear to hear of their plight.

But they cannot listen to you all day, so can they help you in some other way?
Friendship is not a one-way street, you know. There are times when it is more important to be a friend than to have a friend. I repeat: "There are times when it is more important to be a friend than to have a friend. It is in giving that we receive," and surely, "In receiving we are helping a friend to give."

There is an old saying that we must let others do good things for us. "We must not take the good out of their offerings" by even saying, "You should not have." "Helping others not only leads to them helping you, it has its own reward waiting even for them."

How much joy would there be on a birthday or holiday if you do not give of yourself?
Since when does giving a gift or helping a friend not give even you, the giver, a tiny bit of joy?

Our Sons, Daughters, and Immortality

What do you say about the title above? Was it written out of love? Does it really take into consideration the notion of life everlasting? Is it just a thought and can be proven at least by observation? Or do you say that in all of life today, death is always the end? How can it be that there is life after death except within philosophy or religion?

First of all, it is axiomatic in science today that matter cannot be created or destroyed. Its form can only be changed. That includes all living things—all animals, all vegetation, all things that can and should be categorized as living.

I don't want to be morbid, but you can see that except for you and for me (humans), others are consumed by the living as food. But wait, it does include you and me if, for instance, if we were left out on the ground. We then would be consumed by the living. Whether it is wild animal or a domestic dog means nothing. There is no waste; nothing is lost. We can easily see it even in our lives.

A bison will consume tons of grass in its lifetime and convert the plant life into animal protein. The wolf cannot convert the plant into the protein it needs for life, so he feasts on the animal protein of the bison. A bison may have been caught by the pack of wolves and no longer resembles a bison, but he might be part of the eight satiated wolves leaving the scene of the life-and-death struggle.

You and I face a death that is common to all living things, but we live on in the hearts of our offspring, relatives, and friends. Of course, our offspring carry some of our physical and mental characteristics through their genes. But all we come in contact with in our life will also share in our being.

As teachers, we will be a special part of our students' lives. Especially the ones with whom we feel a special bond. Their future undertakings will probably reflect something we have taught them, be it a formal teaching or an informal observation they experienced while with us. They may not even be aware of our influence but have made it part of their personality.

Our friends are especially vulnerable to our influence. Being friends, they have a closer and more intimate relationship with us than do acquaintances. They, like us, have respect for others, and in human relationships, we tend, from early childhood, to mimic the actions of those we like and respect.

So like it or not, and intentional or not, we will live on through others for at least one more generation and possibly more than that. We must remember that we will live on within someone else after we die. Our actions—good and bad—and our inactions—intentional or unintentional—what we taught formally or informally will all live on. Whether we were married or single, solitary or a gregarious leader or follower, we will live on. We have immortality.

Heroes Big and Heroes Small

Yes, we all know heroes in our time. Usually from the military, such as
    Murphy, Basilone, and Kelly.
Some gave their all and some just parts of themselves.
And some seemed to give nothing to join the ranks of heroes.

But there are other heroes in our lives. Some are fathers, brothers,
    mothers, and wives.
Some are part of our folklore: Pitcher, Currie, Nightingale, and more.
Some have given their all in a far-off land. Some are even part of our lives.
Some have heard music and speeches, while others never get the praise.

Some have saved our lives and given theirs.
Some have acted at a moment's notice, and some have toiled for decades
    or for years.
All part of the army of men and women that I can put on a list of people
    who are special.
They are all part of heroes big and heroes small.

But they are not different from you or I. They don't just fall from the sky.
They are just like us, but with the special qualities of superior vision and
   special love.
Think of the woman who shields her children from an abusive man.
Think of the father who raises his brood after the mother has died.

Think of the wife or daughter who give up years to tend to an elderly
   parent to the end.
Or even the girl who leaves her love to minister to her mother, suffering
   from Alzheimer's.
What about the talented musician who give it all up to shovel coal for
   his family?
Or the aunt who becomes the special angel to her deceased sister's
   children.

There are thousands of stories that make our ranks of heroes.
Little stories about simple people who became heroes in their lives.
Who really made us who we are or who we will become?
Who get nothing of the world of acclaim, but gave their all for us just the
   same.

But they are heroes still and will always be honored by you and me.
Not with parades or holidays or sales, but with good works and acts of
   love galore.
A few will join the ranks of heroes. A few will pick up the gauntlet in
   silence and in love.
Repay their gift with our gift of love, and we will become a hero ourselves.

The Purple Band around My Wrist

It's not a charm. It is a message to the world: "Do Not Resuscitate."
It is meant to be what is best for me.
It tells the world exactly what I want,
Not what they want or would like for me.

There are times when my life seems to be at an end.
There are times when the end seems a long way away.
When pain and suffering are leading to nothing
But more suffering and pain.

Science can do wonders today.
It can keep me alive and suffering with almost no end.
Here I am, helpless as I lie
Waiting for my judgment day.

But only a miracle can pick me up.
And we know there are not too many miracles these days.
We know they are few and far between.
We know there comes a time when we are done.

When he is the only one to help us this day.
When we have exhausted every way to stay alive.
All that is left is one more step.
One more step into eternity.

So why do you panic when you see the purple band upon my wrist?
It is there because I have said, "No more, please."
I have run the race; I have given it my all.
Now all that is left is to step into his wonderful hall.

So let me go. Let me be. Let me say what is best for me.
Let me have my dignity. I thank God for my life.
I have met every strife, and now I am spent.
I want to go home to his beautiful tent.

So I go with a smile, and I'll see you there.
When it is your turn to look upon your wrist
And see the purple band, that's your voice saying,
"I am ready to go. I have made my choice."

Who Is Lost—You or I?

I wonder what a casual, invisible observer might think of this situation. It came to my mind last week as I moved into a new senior citizen's home.

The observer might see me sitting on the edge of the bed and considering the last seven inches my feet have to travel before reaching the floor. Would I maintain, or regain, my balance after I hit the floor? Or would I make a grand entrance into my new room and require an accident report to be written? Falling out of bed is frowned on in this establishment. No matter. If not this time, maybe next.

My son and daughter have been unpacking and putting away my clothes and a few mementoes of a wonderful life and marriage. Not too much fit into the one suitcase I had. A few pictures, my old Yankee hat, the key to my old office, and my last birthday cards.

I thought I had been navigating the world around me pretty well for over eighty years. Lately, I have not fallen, even though the stock market, the CD rates, and Social Security rates have taken a tumble. My pension is even almost belly up. I could lose my driver's license and, therefore, the use of my car. Fortunately, I can walk to the coffee shop and visit with my buddies over our morning coffee. It is a small town, and I can walk to almost anything.

I have been able to keep a cheery attitude mainly because I have learned to let my children make most of my decisions and not fight them. Occasionally, I try to envision my future, but I see nothing. Well almost nothing. Maybe doctors and hospital beds and little else. It is when I can see my children and grandchildren that things look the best, and my cheery attitude comes back.

My daughter, who is very busy taking care of my details, and my sons love to talk baseball with me. But somehow even with them, I feel lost and kind of out of the loop. As long as I can remember some little things, everything goes okay. It is when I forget a date of a recent birthday or a player's batting average that I get into trouble. That's when they remind me I am getting old and forgetful.

I was thinking about it yesterday, when they failed to show up with my backpack and they came today, they said they forgot it. Is that the same kind of forget that I do when I forget something? Or is it an indication, like they say to me, that I have lost my way and can no longer be trusted.

I don't say they lost their way when they forget to show up or forget something they promised to bring. I am just happy to see them.

Tell me, dear observer, is it I who have lost my way?

Change Is Constant

I have decided to go with the flow whenever I can. I cannot fight everything. I think I am getting weary of the battles and need to lighten up just to survive.

I am not too sure I am any better off by trying to make things better. Of course "better" means the way *I* want them to be. I may just be making them worse for me and those around me. Maybe this is just a whim that I have this morning, and it will pass. Time will surely tell.

But you, my friend, I cannot forget. I can only imagine the wonderful days when we are close together. Well, "Time will tell." I usually say in difficult situations like this that I am like the fisherman on the shore, and he puts his problems and desires on the hook and casts them into the sea, symbolically giving them to God in the hope they will be solved. Unfortunately, I am really like a fisherman, and I am constantly reeling in the line to check on the progress. I try to cast it into a "better" place for a "better" response.

I might accomplish more just running into the sea and grabbing the problem I want solved, dragging it back to shore, and taking care of it myself. Of course, I might drown, or it might be bigger than me and, as on land, sometimes the bear wins and sometimes the man wins.

On the other hand, I might get a better look at my desires and be energized to fight harder. Or I might see it as being too much for me, and just crawl back to shore, eat some sand, and dream about what could have been. But then I would "a quitter be," and I gave that option up many years ago.

If I live long enough, I may see this as a new beginning and chance for us to be together. But if I die before it is resolved, it is unfortunately your problem to work out by yourself. My fervent hope is that even without the heaven I seek for us, we will at least be happy and good for each other. Supportive of each other along the way—if only as someone too far away to really help but with whom we can verbally share the problems of life.

If you see some bait floating in the sea, be careful. My hook might be inside.

It Is Not What We Get, but What We Give

Oh, you think that I have it wrong.
You think that it is what we get that is best and not what we give.
Let's go back a little way, and see what your joy really looks like.

Remember when the kids were small and loved the holidays?
How they screamed and jumped with every new toy.
You will admit that they were very happy when they got a gift.

But think about a few years later, when they could give you something
    instead.
How they were anxious to see how you liked what they had for you.
The sparkle in their eyes ... the wringing of their hands in anticipation.

Sometimes they were so anxious to give the gift that they tried to give it
   day or two early.
They even played games with their mom to lengthen the good feeling.
They dropped little, "subtle" hints the day before.

And if their gift was something they made, they told and retold how they
   made it.
Yes, they were happier by far to give ... than to receive.
These are the little ones who give from their heart.

These are the little ones who had not been changed by our culture.
They were like you and me, before we learned our "selfish ways."
Before the avalanche of commercials "matured" us.

They were still naive and just full of love.
Yes, we could learn a lesson from them on how to live.
It is not what we get ... but what we give.

Seniors in General

We are not yet dead. But society is pushing us. Just as it takes a village
to make a child into an adult, it seems it also takes a village to make
an adult into a "senior." We all know we respond to subtleties without
realizing it. Family, education (early and late), peers, friends, and life in
general all play a definite role in our formation into adults as well as into
seniors.

During our formative years, we are exposed to the gentle and, at times
hidden nudges of our parents and family. We learn the mores of the
tribe, so to speak. We learn not only what our role is and what is
expected of us, but we also learn the things we should not do.

Men learn from the men around them what is expected of them as men,
and by the same process, women learn what is expected of them as
women from women. Straying too far from the norm brings little nudges,

gentle (and boring) talks, detention, poor grades, and for the more serious deviations, time in jail.

Most, if not all, of these lessons make for a better and happier life. They help us to cope with would-be disasters and generally make for, at the very least, a smoother relationship with those around us. But this education has a less-benign outcome. Yes, just as the process helped us to grow, it also "helps" us age.

We have all heard the admonition, "Act your age." This is especially true when we occasionally act younger than we are. The times we seek a little mental relief and relaxation are when we slip into an already passed age of life. But who is to say what age of life we should be in at any given time? There are no written rules or sequences that we must follow. Yet punishment is to a degree meted out in a series of progressive steps. There is a more damaging and less obvious lesson that we learn, especially regarding aging.

Firstly, our levels of physical and mental activity are usually determined by others to be closely related to our age. Once we pass a certain hidden marker, our experiences and advice no longer have any value. Just as when we were young, our advice was rejected just because we were too young, so, too, later years brings rejection just because we are too old.

Secondly, the push of everyday life removes the patience that seniors need to be afforded to them. Because of slower mental recall and greater volume of experience, it takes longer for us to organize our responses. It is usually forgotten that many of the greatest books, pieces of art, scientific and medical discoveries, and music have been created by seniors.

Thirdly, there is also a subtle nudging into physical inactivity because of our age. Never mind that continued activity is the best process by which seniors stay healthy. It is also the best way to avoid not only several degenerative diseases but life-threatening accidents of everyday living.

Yes, we gain advantages as we age. Most younger people are more tolerant of us, more helpful, and show us a little more respect because of our age. Enjoy it, because it is about the only concession to our age that we will get.

With regard to "old man walking," our ability to walk and maintain our balance is directly related to our general physical condition. It is a good indicator of general health, and as such, it is watched closely by your doctor. The condition of the long muscles of the legs reflect one's health in general and strength and stamina in particular. Yes, doctors always urge you to walk as much as you can.

Yes, while there are advantages as we age, too often we see a lack of patience with, and the rushing of seniors who are on a shopping trip with their children. Granted that when we were young and took care of our children, the future held a much better outcome of growth and maturity than that of a failing senior today, but the outcome is better if seniors can stay active and involved.

No, not Mars—just Alaska as seen from the ship

Friendship — Chapter 4

Today I Saw a Friend

He is just a shell of a man.
Imagine that please, if you can.
He spent his day looking around to see
If he could even remember me.

A few friends for lunch.

Gone is the spring from in his step.
All he could think to do was take another nap.
Well, really that and eating another piece of cake.
Those two things his day would make.

Old age has stolen his vigor and vim.
I wasn't sure it could possibly be him.
He looks like my friend, you see.
He had always been a joy to me.

He was a fine and upstanding fellow.
He was bright and articulate—now he is only mellow.
Now that the years have taken their due,
He is dull when he speaks to you.

Gone is the sparkle from his eye.
He could not even remember to say good-bye.
I saw my friend today.
And I had to look the other way.

A Pair of Mugs

Can you see two mugs on the shelf?
One is for you, and one is for me.
Please look at two mugs on a shelf,
Just waiting to serve both of us.

Let's look at them together and see if they have a story to tell.
Two mugs, side by side, waiting to be held by you and me.
So what will it be, my friend, coffee or tea.
It is morning, and the mugs will be in our hands.

But this is only the beginning of their service to us.
They help us at lunch and dinner each day.
They can even help us snack before we say good night.
Then, for sure, you will not catch me looking over the edge.

Time to relax, so down come the faithful mugs.
Out come the snacks, and to our places at the table.
A little party for two, no four. You and I and our two mugs, you see.
We share our days and nights in happy serenity,

And looking at you with your beauty right next to me.
Let's leave the mugs on the table and go inside before we retire.
The mugs are holding some Irish whiskey tonight.
That means sleep and fond dreams will surely transpire.

Earlier today, after picking up pinecones in an autumn breeze,
The cups held hot chocolate and floating marshmallows.
But still they seem to say that you and I should get closer each day.
We, as they, are happiest when we are side by side.

Choose Your New Beau

Give yourself credit where credit is due.
God even seems to think that your new beau will be special for you.
Your beau is not perfect, but neither is anyone else I can see.
You will find that your new beau is better just for you.

Almost anything you do is better for two,
From taking a walk to a smile or a kiss.
All through the day, he is someone you will miss.
And when things get rough, he will be there for you.

He is someone to get the sugar, even the mail when it rains.
He is someone to share the good and the bad.
He is someone to take your wrath when you get mad.
But best of all he is someone to love and who loves you in return.

Dear Special, Longtime Friend

How can we still be friends after all these years?
How can all this still be true?
How can we wash away all the tears?
How can you like me, and I still like you?

There must be something special we see in each other.
There must be something deep inside.
There must be a unique feeling that time cannot smother?
There must be a place where only we reside.

But now the years seem to have passed us by.
And we can only sit and ask him why.
Even though life has been sometimes down and sometimes up,
Could it be that we can still drink of the friendship cup?

Could we still feel a special bond?
Could we still feel that there is no other?
Could we still feel happy with what we have found?
Could we still want the other to be around?

Can we laugh and share together the good things of the day?
Can we empathize and sympathize with each other?
Can we listen, and can we still have our say?
Can we support the foibles of one another?

Is there a path that we can walk?
Is there a need that we can fill?
Is there room for us to talk?
Is there enough caring within us still?

There are questions within me now.
There are problems about our lives.
There are things that I seek to answer somehow.
There are answers we must find to survive.

Hi, Confidante

Though miles may separate us now,
There was a time when life itself pulled us apart.
But as you know, life changes from day to day.
What was good and proper then just did not stay.

There was a period of mourning, which we survived.
But now we have picked ourselves up ... you before me.
And though our memories will sometime make us fuss,
We are finally looking up to see what can really be for us.

With love and friendship for each other,
We have built a new life of understanding.
And, of course, with help from above,
We now can say, "Yes, my friend, you and I."

Favorito Santo

Throughout our life we meet saints in unexpected places.
And some would say, "There are no saints on piano benches."
They never sat before Mrs. K and felt her talent ...
Her wisdom ... her gentleness ... or her love.

Even when week after week we practice scales,
With untrained fingers going astray,
The help and wonders of the lady behind us,
Giving support, love, and correction—all with a gentle touch.

She teaches music sprinkled with self-respect.
She teaches honor and the joy of music's gift.
She teaches us to hear the birds and see the sky.
All because Mrs. K has us under her spell.

Even when puppy love puts us in distress,
Mrs. K has a word and a tissue for our eyes.
She dabs and consoles our heart and soul,
Where the music she has taught us forever lies.

And later, much later, when we are adults,
And if we stop in to take a lesson or two,
Dear Mrs. K is there behind us as before,
With support and loving words of wisdom.

A hundred years is not enough for her.
Mrs. K has put music inside our lives,
To live with love and sweet refrains.
She restores our confidence and our tunes.

But some still say, "There are no saints on piano benches."
I would say that they are wrong ... very wrong.
I was changed forever on her bench.
The piano bench where I met my favorite saint ... Mrs. K.

**Cape May, New Jersey and the Atlantic
Ocean near the Delaware River.**

Short Stories — Chapter 5

The Mystery of Cabin 828

Of all the wonderful inventions of society, the cruise ship is one of the greatest. It is a relatively new retreat for me and experienced only since my wife died. The wonderful atmosphere created on a ship by the separation from everyday life and its many problems is refreshing.

A cruise ship similar to the ship in "The Mystery of Cabin 828."

This world, with its emphasis on relaxation and entertainment, is very intoxicating. Some landlubbers think the gently swaying of the ship and the throbbing of the engines create an atmosphere of unsteadiness, but to me, it is like the pulsating heart of the woman one is holding close. That kind of relationship does not come with the ticket, but there is always the possibility. Or so the literature says.

This being only my third cruise, I have yet to master all the intricacies of forming new relationships. The woman in the next cabin came out at the same time as I did, and we walked together for a while in the evening breezes. Then we stopped in a little lounge over the bow of the ship. And after a few, very few, drinks, we realized we had experienced recent losses. Our nodding acquaintance moved on to an informal sharing of the view and a drink, and we parted for the night. As I lay in my cabin, remembering the happenings of the day, it occurred to me that the parting smile might have held a little more than an, "I am sorry you are leaving," message.

What the heck. "You only live once," now having new and personal meaning to me, gave me the nerve to get up. After dressing, I knocked on her cabin door, number 828. We went back out, strolled the deck, and poured out our hearts again to each other. This was possible because we did not know each other and would probably never meet again.

Eventually, we were standing by her cabin door and again saying good night. And again she said the "I am sorry you are leaving" speech. This time I had the nerve to say, "I have a bottle of wine in my cabin," and should we go there. That did not go over too well, and I retreated quickly to, "I'll get my wine and be back in a minute."

As I went into my cabin, I had a million thoughts and two million "lines" I could use. Carrying the bottle and two glasses, I left my cabin and turned toward the bow and her cabin. But there was no number on the door next to mine. Befuddled, I retraced my steps and even went toward the stern. Still no number 828. There were only service closets on either side of me. *Now what?* I thought.

Back in my room, I put down the glasses and reluctantly put on my pajamas again. Even the room layout on the door for the escape route in case of a fire had room 828 next to mine. After putting on my robe and checking the numbers on the doors next to me, again finding no number 828, I went back to my room.

While I was contemplating this mysterious happening, a note was slipped under my door. It was the nightly blurb concerning recreational opportunities for the next day. It was folded so the room number appeared on the outside: "Number 828." I crumpled it up and threw it into the wastebasket, only to retrieve it the moment it hit the bottom. I opened the slip up again to read the room number, and now it read room 826. A sip, or two or three, of the wine seemed just right about now, though not exactly what I originally had in mind.

As my head settled softly onto the pillow, I felt the gentle swaying of the ship and the throbbing of the engines. I soon drifted off, but I first experienced a little presleep shiver and suddenly had a fleeting sense of my wife in heaven, laughing at my plight.

First Bacon

We have all heard of the dog named Shep. There was a bond between Shep and old Tom Patterson that was closer than most. Many a snowy morning they could be seen walking on their early morning rounds. They started at their home, went to the corner, and turned up Chancellor Street to the fish market. But wait, let them tell it themselves.

We like to walk past the fish market, well not the fish market (a little odorous you know) but the butcher shop next door. Usually at about 8:15, a coffeepot was set outside the back door, and Jake would invite all who came by to have a nice cup of hot coffee plus a fresh bun from Sophie's Bakery up the street. That is also the best place to get the early morning scuttlebutt concerning happenings the night before. There was usually nothing much going on in a small town such as Cranford. But occasionally, as happened last week, someone hits a parked car at the bend in the road, and Mike Jones had a little too much beer and had to sleep it off at the "hotel," compliments of the police chief.

There's Sam, a fireman, putting out the flag in front of the firehouse. The area looks nice and clean, since they put up that new memorial to the forces fighting in the too many wars around the world. We next go past the town clock, where we usually sit and watch the commuters line up in the tunnel under that train tracks, waiting for the express bus to New York. Funny thing about that line. Oh, it is very orderly for sure, but it is also stone silent. No one talks at all while in line. The last time someone spoke on that line before the 6:30 bus was when Mrs. Smith had her first daughter three years ago. That was the first girl born into the Smith family in two generations. Carl Smith was happily giving out cigars to the people on line.

We turn right here and cut through the gas station. Sunday this is a mob scene, with everyone in town picking up their enlarged Sunday papers and then scurrying off to church. A quick stop at Mrs. Kimmel's next door. Because she has difficulty navigating the front steps, we pick her paper off the grass and put it on the porch for her.

Well, here we are, back to our street. I can smell the bacon and eggs on the stove even from a block away. Tom would reach down and take the leash off of me, so I could run at full speed up the driveway and wait for him on the porch. My tail would clear all the snow off the top step, and as soon as he opened the door, I would beat him down the hall into the kitchen for the first piece of bacon. Most days are not what Tom would call "dog" days, but after our morning walk ... that is exactly what I would call it.

The Blue Coat

Much has been said about my sitting by the window.
My boys complain that I am spoiling their games.
They can't play freely because of me.
They must watch their language when I am around.
They can't fool with the girls and tease them when I watch.

But what about me. My house is clean, and supper gets done.
I am home alone, and people interest me.
New York's Upper East Side is full of stories and mystery.
I can watch the peddlers in the street.
They sell fish, fruits, and ice all day.
I watch the girls play double Dutch.

While the boys like to play stickball and kick the can.
There's not much work for them these summer days.
But once in a while, some strangers come upon the scene.
They push and shove my neighbors around.
Their main job is to stay out of trouble.
The gangs have not taken over the street nor drug dealers do you meet.
Then parents come out and keep the peace or call the police.
It is August, and it is hot, a real New York summer day.
Hot and humid, and a blazing sun beats down on all.

Some have left the pavement to find some shade.
I see a crowd of kids and some pushing and shoving.
They all have bandanas and white T-shirts.
There are more of them than anyone else.
They are not from our neighborhood.

Here comes a girl out of the subway a block away.
To reach the street she must run a gauntlet.
There she goes and is doing fine ... a few more feet, and she will be safe.
Oh, she tripped, and now they are all around, and she is on the ground.
What should I do? What should I do? Should I call the police?
I never want to get involved. What should I do?
It was a girl with a blue coat in a shopping bag.

Then I see a boy hold up the bag she was carrying.
They took it from her and are tearing it apart.

Oh, how I hate when they play keep-away.
Out falls a blue winter coat.
She looks frantic ... there is blood on her head.
The police are here and have grabbed some guys.
The ambulance has arrived and has taken the girl away.

Oh my God, there's Lisa, my fourteen-year-old.
She has a purse and is coming this way.
She comes up the stairs and shows it to me.
She thinks it belongs to the girl with the blue coat.
That was my Millie, walking through the gang.

As the thought that I could have helped my daughter
Pushes all other thoughts away, a policeman rushes up the
Stairs, looking for the lady who sits in the window.
Millie wants me to pick up the blue coat at the hospital to keep it safe
While she recuperates from her injuries.

Finally, Amy Is Safe

Our family album starts when we brought little Amy home from the
hospital after her birth. She was so tiny, so dependent on us. She was
so small (5 pounds, 1 ounce) that we had to feed her every two hours,
And then, she could only hold an ounce or two of formula at one time.
We never did learn how to avoid the nipples clogging in the middle of
the night. We would scurry around, trying to restart the flow to satisfy
Amy's hunger.

She was playful as a child and loved a "swing" made by her daddy's arms
going back and forth and sometimes very high. I can still hear her giggles
and her joy on her favorite ride. Then it stopped. When she was about
five years old (almost too big for the swing), she would shy away and
make excuses not to ride.

There were other things happening, too. Amy wanted her light on all night. She wanted me to read to her every night until she fell asleep. And then one night, after her daddy read to her, or so I thought, she had a night terror. I found blood on her sheets. A terrible night, full of screams and tears. I held her close and rocked her until morning, when she finally fell back to sleep.

After I made breakfast and Tom was off to work, I went up and found Amy curled in a tight ball on her bed, sobbing quietly. We talked and talked, and finally she told me how daddy would not read to her but would get into bed with her and play some terrible games. I felt awful for her. I felt as though I had failed as her mother to protect her from that evil.

That night I sent Amy to have supper at her friend's house. When Tom came home, I confronted him. We screamed and argued. I cried, "How could you?" Of course, he had no answer except to say she reminded him of me, with her golden hair and cute smile. He never left the table alive. The police came and took me away. I was released a few months later. At the trial, they ruled, "justifiable homicide."

Then, with Amy back home and in our routine of life, we were closer than ever. But she cried each night and slept with the light on. She was afraid of all men and clung to me so that I could hardly walk. She had no girlfriends, and her grades in school slipped to a new low each marking period. Amy's visits to her child psychologist only produced more tears and more reports that it would take more time, and more time, and more time. "She might never be normal again," they said.

That is when I knew what I had to do for Amy. I scoured the newspapers and the internet every night, looking for a small town where I am either close enough to a big city to get Amy the best possible health care and still have a small-town ambiance, or at least have a regional health-care facility in the town.

I realize it requires my getting a new job, Amy going to a new school with all new friends, and, in effect, starting all over again. I would even change all the furniture and get new clothes for Amy. As frightening and complicated as it sounds, I want to give Amy a new start, without the hundreds of little things to remind her of her past experiences.

Now, I am again rocking my smiling Amy and assuring her that her daddy will never, ever hurt her again.

Aliens Invade Revelers

It seems there is now evidence aliens have been walking on earth for hundreds of years. It is amazing that no one has seen them or recognized they are around. It is also amazing they have been studying us for so long without our knowing it. Let us look at the evidence.

A group of scientists were excavating around some Pueblo ruins and came across the remains of a dinosaur family that apparently was caught in a flash flood and drowned. The amazing thing is that they also found the remains of some human hunters in a nearby strata, where the hunters were also caught in a flood a few thousand years later. The dinosaur find was enough for them to be happy, but the finding of human remains in the same area was even more astonishing.

It was apparently a hunting party of four or five hunters. But among the regular items one would expect to find with a hunting party, such as a spear and a club, they also found a metal cylinder that was fashioned by a much more technologically advanced group. It was five inches long and the size of a C-battery flashlight. There were caps of some kind on each end, but they were not screwed on. The item was cataloged as being from a different era, which indicated it was not one site but two.

On examining the artifacts at the university, it was surprising to find the cylinder was emitting some radioactivity, indicating it had not originated in the valley where it was discovered. They also found they could not identify the metal or metal-like material from which it was constructed. Its composition did not conform to metals or plastics found on earth. X-ray examination revealed there was a special latch, much like a hidden

Chinese latch from the Ming Dynasty, that would release the ends of the container. Inside was a square metal bar, three inches long, and with what appeared to be a computer chip embedded in the center.

It took four years to extract the chip and find that, unlike electrical circuits common to computers today, it was a maze of miniature hollow passageways of various lengths. It was only two microns thick and had a reducing spiral shape of a conch of the Strombus Era and interconnected at each end in what appeared in a haphazard fashion. After mapping the passages and feeding the results into a supercomputer, scientists realized it was not a haphazard layout but a sequence of variously sized dots, similar to Morse code. Plus, there were repeating sequences, as would be found in a message.

Three more years of study found the dots made up instructions for entering the minds of human beings (usually when the humans are not preoccupied with their work and had been drinking alcohol) and taking over their thinking and physical activities. The message also said the procedure was not without bugs, and much more research had to be done to the subjects (humans) to be of any value to the aliens.

While being studied, it was reported that the subjects (humans) had difficulty speaking without slurred speech, reduced motor functions, difficulty walking straight, and an inability to focus on instructions. Some even became combative, and all seemed to lose their sense of right and wrong. It was also reported there was no known antidote for the libation, but that after a good night's sleep, the humans recovered completely with only 12 percent suffering headaches or nausea. There could also be some long-term problems, such as early onset dementia, weight gain, and liver damage. This was especially true for men.

Of course, this has led to a worldwide study of ten thousand patients, who also occasionally suffered with these symptoms of impaired balance, slurred speech, aggressiveness, sleepiness, and even jealousy. The study would ascertain what induced such a state and whatever else they had in common. It is expected that the study will take at least eight years to complete.

If you have experienced any of the described symptoms or have any idea as to the cause and/or a possible antidote, please share your findings with the author.

Two Sloops at Sea

Yes, we sailed the great ocean, you see, my sister and me.
Together, but a few yards apart, we braved the sea to see the world one
    wave at a time.
To go from crest to crest and trough to trough, and tacking our way
    cross the brine.
We sailed from East to West and from North to South—always side by
    side.

We were in two sloops, one for her and one for me, as we traversed the
    wonderful sea.
Going first to port and then to starboard, my sister and me.
At times we left the haven at the end of the road with sun and calm sea.
But after a while, the weather would change, and we were tossed about.

We thought we were brave, but in reality, we were foolish to sail alone.
The sea is no place for two women so far from their home.
But as we grew we learned, using trial and error.
We came to be sailors and controlled our terror.

First we sailed within the bay, and only a few hours would we stay.
Always watching the sky and the sea for signs of trouble.
We watched the currents and watched the clouds.
To find our way, we read the birds by day and the stars by night.

Each night back to home, to beds that did not sway.
To a warm drink and good food that was always there for us.
To clean up and then to plan for tomorrow's foray
To Mother Nature's vast and wonderful sea.

Peaceful at times, but fickle and then angry at our intrusion.
With crashing waves and howling winds.
With tossing about and spinning around.
With straining and hauling and pulling of lines.

With prayers to the good Lord as to why we came out.
Why did we leave the peace and calm?
Why did we take such chances I thought ... then with one crashing
    wave,
With screams and shouts of dismay ... then silence.

Not two sloops upon the water, only one and one frightened lass.
One lonely and frightened woman, fighting the turmoil.
Searching the waves and the wind for her sister alive.
I was the only one left of ... my sister and me.
But I refused to give my sister to the waves.

I refused to leave my sister here in the boiling sea.
One more come-around and one more crest to top.
One more trough to cross, and finally, near exhaustion,
I caught a glimpse of something orange in the sea.

Yes, yes, it was my sister's life preserver, doing its job.
Holding her head above the water until I could come around.
And come around I did. I did everything just right.
I had my sister alongside and in my dinghy in a flash.

Giving her, and me, another chance
There was an ambulance waiting at the dock.
A quick trip to the hospital and then the ride home.
As we sat sipping tea, I printed a "For Sale" sign for my sloop.

No Dreams, Please

It seems to me that the "cleansing" of the Cambodian people and the enforcing of Angka was going as well as could be expected. The Khmer Rouge rid itself of the label of being a band of criminals and become a legitimate political party. The redistribution of the wealth of the nation in a more equitable manner required that the population be reduced by about two million people.

There was a great need for the likes of myself and my twin brother. We organized the reduction of the population into manageable units, and we saw some success in the resulting numbers. Unfortunately, even though we were dedicated to the program, it did take an emotional toll even on us. Death was all around us. The disposal of the bodies was always a difficult problem.

And now, sixty years later, I see ways in which we could have been more efficient. But the program is over, and the Khmer Rouge is gone. Some of our leaders have been tried, convicted, and put to death. My brother and I are now awaiting trial. Unfortunately, or fortunately, my brother has Parkinson's dementia and cannot tell where his dreams end and his reality begins. He is in a constant state of confusion. I am happy to say I do not suffer from that malady.

My room, or cell, is adequate, and I have a nice bed on which to sleep. I usually fall asleep quickly, and even though I have a recurring dream concerning our activities, I awake each morning feeling refreshed. For instance, in my dream last night, we "eliminated" a prominent family. It was from about the same economic level as our family. Normally, if one could say what we did was "normal," our whole family would have met its death on a summer afternoon in the fields of Cambodia. But because of our prominence in the movement, we had been protected from harm. So far.

In my recurring dream, I am, as usual, overseeing the deaths for the afternoon and disposal of the bodies. The chaos of the killing still rings in my ears, as do the brutal scenes of the afternoon. Usually, I wake up to the sounds and smells of a new day ... leaving my dreams behind.

But today, things went a little differently. Instead of a brightening of the sky, the singing of birds, and the smells of breakfast, my dream abruptly changed with the jailers bursting into my room and my arrest. But no matter. A dream is a dream, and there would be no consequences.

I cannot shake the sounds, turmoil, and jostling of the "Killing Fields." I have been taken to a regular prison cell during the night. Right now, there seems to be a hearing outside my cell, and a legal proceeding is taking place.

I am getting a little upset with my dream, and I hope I wake up soon. I would love a little tea and a rice cake. They stand me up, and I am led into the prison yard. A sentence of "Hang by the neck until dead" is read. They put a hood over my head. My last view is of my brother, smiling in the corner. I scream to him, "I want to wake up … now." I am forced to stand on a shipping crate with the noose around my neck. I scream, "I want to wake up! Please! Wake me up … now! A soldier pulls the shipping crate from under my feet, and I drop. I hold my breath, waiting for the jolt. But it did not come. Or did I just not feel it.

13D—Willie's Favorite Seat

Seat 13D, Sun-Up Airlines, departing Raleigh–Durham, North Carolina, on Monday at 8:00 a.m. This schedule allows Willie plenty of time to make his sales calls to clients in the New Jersey area before his return flight to RDU on Tuesday evening.

Willie always books the same center seat in the last row—13D—and remains glued in it until he reaches his destination. However, today Willie is on a new medication and needs to make one more stop at the restroom. Unfortunately, his "safe" seat is in the last row, and the lavatories on this plane are in the front of the cabin.

To the casual observer, Willie appears to be calm, but inside, he is in terrible turmoil. According to his wife, he has been reading too many mechanic's books about the history of airplane mechanical defects and passenger safety. He has convinced himself (and anyone who will listen) that his research has indicated this airplane has had its share of problems.

As Willie is walking to his assigned seat (speaking to no one in particular), he says out loud, "Can you believe this plane is over twenty-five years old and has been owned by three different airlines so far? Not only that, two of the previous owners farmed out all of their maintenance. In fact, this plane had two incidents of skidding off the runway during landing!"

Just then, Willie hears over the intercom, "Ladies and gentlemen, please set your seats to their upright position, raise your food tray, and fasten your seat belt. We are about to start our descent."

Willie decides to make one more quick trip to the restroom before the landing. *Wow! This is a hard landing ... Why aren't we slowing down? Actually, it feels as though we are speeding up ... no reverse thrust ... no braking. Now the plane has veered to the left and is going off the runway!* Willie is anxious to get to his safe seat in the rear of the plane before the inevitable happens.

Finally, the plane skids to a stop. Luckily, there is no fire! "Please, help me get out of here," Willie pleads as he struggles to get off the deck after falling while coming out of the front restroom. Willie's heart pulsates as he tries to run, but his legs are sluggish and heavy, and he can't move. He is shaking and perspiring profusely as he tries to escape. A good samaritan is urgently trying to lift him to his feet.

Willie is startled to hear his wife's voice anxiously asking, "Willie, Willie, what happened? Have you fallen out of bed again? If you don't get up now, you'll miss your flight!"

Frozen Mustang

I was checking the sky behind me to see if any of the planes were trying a last-minute maneuver to beat me to the flag. Possibly diving out of the sun and pulling up inches above the water to drain the last Gs off the wings. But there were none.

My P-51, named *Glacier Maiden*, had performed flawlessly after fifty years below the ice in Alaska and now was faster and better than when it was new. I know my course was a variation of the Great Circle Route, and although it appeared longer on the map, it was really miles shorter.

I also had removed my "P" tube, which added two miles per hour to my top speed. Luckily, I had remembered not to take my water pill before I left, or I would have been in big trouble.

The danger, which I accepted, was that I could easily slip into Mach 1 on any descent and lose it all. I had to be careful to watch my altimeter and keep above 100 feet above sea level and my air speed below 525 knots. I had remembered to reset my altimeter, as I did not have radar assist.

The race officials had warned us of turbulence over Denver, but fortunately, I found the jet stream there and was able to lose only 125 miles of distance. It was actually the same situation I had encountered when flying on a speed run with my SR-71 while in the air force (Colonel John "Smiling Jack" Smith). Then, I had been able to use a "hole" for my fifth refueling.

Now I must concentrate and get into my final maneuver with the last vertical pull-up, slide off, and descend to the runway. Here we go. Nice wing over. Good ... Good ... Now back slide, drop off, and down I go ... 521 knots, altitude 700 feet ... 523 knots ... Altitude 452 feet ... 525 knots. A little buffeting. Stick is getting heavy. Reverse stick (up is now down, and down is now up). Careful ... careful. I wonder if my wife is watching. I lost my focus for about four seconds.

Damn! I went through 538 knots. Altitude 190 feet. I hope this baby can take it during the pull-up.

Buzz, ring, buzz, ring. The warning alarm blared, "Ship is exceeding Mach 1 [speed of sound] and over 8 Gs on main frame." There is a real possibility the ship will break up.
More buffeting ... Wind ... Silence.

"Ladies and gentlemen, the latest report concerning the pilot is that he did not survive. His wife said she was happy he died doing what he loved to do, and she would take a train back to New Jersey for his funeral."

Continuous Evaluation

What is all this noise about over-testing our children? Do we want to prepare them for life, or do we not? What is life without a test or two each and every minute of the day? Before you got out of bed, your body had been performing tests on itself all night to see if you can breath enough, stand up, and walk to the bathroom. It has tested many parts and functions without you knowing it. There are times when you will say, even before opening your eyes, "I cannot get up today. I must be getting the flu." Your evaluation is based on subconscious testing of your body even before you put your feet on the floor.

Testing means life ... testing means progress ... testing means you are learning and moving ahead. When you kiss your wife good morning, you are subconsciously looking for affirmation that she still loves you and wants to be with you. Yes, you have already passed an important test.

Okay, you both passed your morning tests and are still together. But now at work, has the testing stopped? My friend, your testing has just begun. Every project you work on, every job your boss gives you to do is a test. Try not getting the project correct or messing up on even a little job, and you will see if you were being tested. I will bet you are always being tested, if not formally then informally.

While at work, try answering the phone to take information down or respond to a request for a product. If you don't get it right, you will find out if you were being tested. Life is unlike baseball, where you can fail to get a hit 70 percent of the time and still be considered a success. Imagine if you failed even 50 percent of the time when your boss gives you an assignment. You are expected to get most things right 100 percent of the time.

So how can one think we can teach our children that testing is not important? If we teach in school that life is just doing things and it makes no difference if you get it right, how are we preparing them for the real world? Life demands being as close to perfection as we can be. Not once in a while, but over and over again, day after day. Are our morals tested only 30 percent of the time or every moment? Is our honesty tested only on Friday night when we get our pay? Can one say that "This is the third Friday of the month, and I can take all the money I want for myself"? Must we tell the truth and not steal at all opportunities or only when we might get caught?

Let us not be harsh with our children, but we must also be sure to give them all the tools they will need when they leave our care. We do them no favor by making their tasks too easy or too harsh. We must prepare them with the skills they need to earn a living and to be honest, productive adults, and testing is a large part of what occurs in business every day.

Topsy-Turvy World

Assuming life begins at thirty years old—
Everything is topsy-turvy
Born rich—die poor.
Born strong—die weak.
Born into a family—die alone.
Born smart—die dumb.
When we are healthy and strong—they kill us in the army.
When we are weak and frail—they let us live.

When we go to school for an education to succeed—we pay our own way.
They say that the school years are our best years—but then they give us
    homework.
When we retire and do not need an education—everything is free.
When we are young and can eat everything—they tell us what to eat.
When we can no longer eat everything—they say eat what you want.
When we are young and virile—we must be in when the streetlights go
    on.
When we are young and look for girls—they are too old for us.
When we are old and look for women—they are too young for us.
When we are older yet—there are more women than men.
When we see a beautiful woman and want to live—they tell us she
    would kill us.
When we think we have it all figured out—we forget.
When we get smart—we are too old.

On the Lighter Side
— Chapter 6

Pasta in Prose

Many years ago (1938) and in another world, or so it seems to me, I lived behind a candy store. Not unusual in those days to live behind a "Mom and Pop" store.

As a child, there could be nothing better. We sold candy, groceries, etc., and I am sure that contributed to my being such a popular guy in the neighborhood. I remember selling cigarettes at two cents apiece—three for a nickel. Though illegal now for a seven-year-old to sell cigarettes, these were Depression days, and the laws were not as sophisticated or enforced as today. I remember selling butter from a tub.

I remember two books behind the counter. One was the "credit" book for our regular customers and their daily purchases to be paid off on Friday evening. My dad and I went to their homes to get our money before it was all spent at the bar across the street.

The other book was the "numbers" book. A customer would try to predict the number for the day at a local racetrack and bet a nickel or a dime and get a slip from the book. In the evening, a bookie would pick up the money and the book with a record of the plays, and the next day, he would bring the winnings, if there were any winners from the previous day. Obviously outside the law, but remember it was the Depression, and everyone needed to be very creative to pay your bills.

It is not unusual for one to remember a food that was a favorite in their childhood and many years later try it again. Most of the time, the food is not exactly as you remember it, and you wonder why you liked it so much.

But not so with orzo and a little milk as a cereal in the morning. There were few breakfast cereals to choose from then and no money to pay for them, so one would naturally go to inexpensive pasta like orzo. It looks like a grain of rice only slightly larger. It is still used in soups.

You and I know very well that most of what we remember from our childhood becomes exaggerated with the passage of time. But believe me when I say that not with my orzo this morning. With a little milk, it was the best I have ever had for breakfast. I was put in a special frame of mind. Better than usual and special.

I am sure that today I will also remember the flat tires going to the shore, sleeping on the bedroom floor on hot summer nights, swimming under the railroad bridge, the terrible scourge of polio, and many other things— both good and bad.

But today I also remember running to the store very early, and with a little metal scoop, taking some orzo from the glass case for my mom to cook for my breakfast.

Today, with orzo in my bowl, at least for a little while, I am a child again.

A Birthday Died Last Year

As a child, we wait in joyful anticipation of a birthday. Yes, we almost
  wish our lives away.
We jump with glee to see our friends.
We are all excited about the gifts and the games that day.
But soon enough, we pass little milestones, and birthdays seem to fade
  away.
They seem to lose their power and importance as we settle into our life
  and say,
"I don't want to celebrate birthdays any longer."
If we are part of a family, the new young ones are the new party ones.
  "We will have a party for Michael, he will be six months old."
And then we start measuring our lives by the progress of their lives. "I
  got that new job the year Timmy was born."
There even comes a time when we deny a birthday has actually passed.
  "I am only thirty-nine"—on our forty-first birthday.
And lo and behold, we seem to add on extra years. "I will be eighty in
  two years."
Then we are proud and think aloud of our collection of birthdays. "I'm
  ninety-three or ninety-four; I can't remember which."
Even after we are gone, our friends and family will celebrate our birthday
  with, "Today would have been Sam's birthday had he lived," or,
  "Mom would have been one hundred today."
That is about as far as it goes, unless of course if we are a celebrity and
  then we never die.
But yes, birthdays die for you and I.

My Lost Checkbook and Me

Where are you my checkbook, my friend?
Are you hiding because I have a computer turned on?
That is progress, so maybe this is our end.
Besides, your money will shortly all be gone.

This being the first of the month and after I pay my rent,
Your contents are sure to be completely spent.
I have raided your account and checks I have sent
To merchants and charities all around.

But its time to dip into your belly
And take out the last few bucks.
There are children who need to be merry,
And dogs and cats to be fed, along with a few birds.

But try as I might, I have still given myself a fright.
Where have you gone, and when will you be back?
I looked where it is dark and looked where it is light.
But you may be hiding behind the old spice rack.

So come out now and show yourself to me.
I am tired of searching. It is getting very late.
I will be happy to see you, and you will be happy to see me.
If you just come out now, I'll clean off our slate.

We have been friends for many a year.
I'll admit that at times I failed to know your balance.
And at times I fear I left you empty and without a penny.
But now you may retire to wherever old checkbooks go.

Good-bye, my friend. It has not always been fun, my only sin was
I tried to squeeze a little more out of you than I had put in.
But you survived the trials that each month did bring, and now
I promise to put you on a shelf and forever keep you dry.

Crushed Arachis Hypogaea

If you had to choose one food that sustains more children in this country than any other, what would you say?

I know you looked at the title of this article and you just said, "Peanut butter." No more cheating. But why? What do most people like about it?

Its color is nothing great to look at. Its taste is debatable? Nothing else is like it. It is not sweet. It does not taste like JELL-O.

If you put it on bread and drop it, the side with it is always the side that lands on the floor, and it is difficult to clean up: especially from a rug. It also stains your homework if it gets within six inches of it. You can check with your child's teacher about that.

Its texture? Not so good, as it usually sticks to the roof of your mouth. Ask your dog.

In fact, you can get it creamy, dry, natural (with oil on top), smooth, and with various sizes of lumps inside. It can be with jelly, without jelly, with butter, without butter, just plain. You buy it, and fix it any way that you like it.

It tastes great spread on a banana, or how about on a banana and bacon sandwich? It goes well with milk, coffee, tea, soda, and even water.

It is a spread, it is in cereals, it is in candy, it is a dip, it is mixed with chocolate, and it is put on cakes. It is inside of cakes and even inside of cookies. It is often mixed in ice cream for a summer treat. In fact, have you ever tried it on a stalk of celery to eat?

It needs no refrigeration and goes on crackers, bread, bagels, pretzels, rolls, and English muffins—and even can be licked directly off your fingers.

It is not too great before a date with a special friend. If you eat it, you might smell like an elephant. (Remember ET?) By the way, the elephant also thinks it is just fine.

If you lived in Thailand, your mom would use it in cooking and as a dip. It is even good licked directly from a spoon.

There is a word of caution I must tell you. There are some people who are very allergic to it, so never offer it to any child without checking with an adult to see if the child can eat it.

PS: I will bet you know a few ways to eat it that I have not mentioned.

Flavored Gelatin

Yes, you heard me clear.
There is nothing better than a dish
Of JELL-O, my dear.
It is the best there is to top off a little knish.

Or any other meal you can choose.
It is the JELL-O that makes it the best.
Have JELL-O, and you cannot lose.
JELL-O perks up all the rest.

Now JELL-O, you know, comes in a great variety
Of flavors and colors for you to choose.
Any special dessert in our society
Is not as good as just plain JELL-O.

What is your favorite, my friend or my friar?
Just buy JELL-O, and you cannot go wrong.
There is color and texture and plenty of flavor.
And it is really as cheap as the proverbial song.

But every time that you want to buy, you must choose.
There is always a flavor that is discounted that day.
There are colors like yellow and red and even blue like the sky.
Whether it is orange or lemon or lime ... or whatever you say.

But the best is not the cost of the flavorful blast.
The best is the flavor that makes you feel great
And brings to you memories of a time long past.
JELL-O was the best no matter what was the rest.

You would eat the food that you would get,
And like a good fellow even lick the bowl.
But JELL-O at the end you will never forget.
As always, "JELL-O is everybody's dessert."

Some Words Are Dead

I think of all the things I could have said.
I think of all the things still in my head.
But if I said all the things still in my head,
Believe me, I would be among the dead.

There are no words that could rescue me.
Nothing, nothing that could save my soul.
For if everything that I could have said
Ever got out of my head ... I surely would be dead.

There are no laws. There are no rules
That could make me pay for what is in my head.
The law says while they are in my head, they are dead.
I must say them to give them being—but then I would be ...

You can see there is only pity for me.
My words not said are in some nether world.
They have no form. They have no life.
The law says they do not exist. They are dead.

My Bagel and Me Can Answer the Call

Or should I have called it, "My Bagel and I"?
Well, never mind, I will not talk about me or I.
This is about the bagel, I will sigh.

Not every invention of man or woman can claim
To have such wonders of taste or fame.
Not to honor it would be a crying shame.

The bagel even has a hole at its center
Through which a carrying pole you may enter.
My favorite bagel is made by Lender.

I hear now there are at least two major classes.
There is a New York bagel that is made for the masses,
And there is the California bagel for the upper classes.

But never mind, because you will find
That both you will eat until there is nothing behind.
They both will nourish you and elevate your mind.

But what, you ask, is their flavor today?
That is where your baker can say
Any flavor you want, "We make it any way."

Of course, there is "plain" or "pumpernickel."
There is "onion" or "salt" and even "garlic" for more than a nickel.
You can probably get "the works" minus a little pickle.

But how much can I say about this special food
That gets you going and in the mood
To take on the world or care for the brood?

I cannot tell you from where they came.
They may have even had a different name.
I am sure you know no two the same.

But they go back in history and can probably claim.
To have saved a nation that was almost slain.
Did I mention cream cheese or butter on toasted or plain?

Octogenarian

Yes, eighty is only a number, but in most circles, it is a large number.
But even if it is a large number, one could say—so what!
It does not have much meaning to you or to me,
Unless we have at least eighty of something special, you see.
It is the thing, not the number that counts.

But what does it matter to a guy like me?
What does one say if he has eighty dollars in his pocket?
I would say I have someone else's pants on.
Yes, fortunate he would say—but only because of what it can buy.
A little food or drink, a tavern "round" you might think.

Maybe even a pair of shoes, if your old pair you did lose.
How about giving at least some of it to charity.
Would that make the wad seem large enough?
Does doing good for others and sharing the joyful roll
Make it better than just some money from a dole?

I will bet you are saying by now that eighty years is great to have.
But eighty years of toil is not what I would want for you or me.
Eighty years of love and friendship is what I have experienced.
Of course, it rained during my life, but now I don't remember when.
Must I be satisfied with the eighty? I have no say, so please go away.

Suppose we make it eighty times two—eighty for me, and eighty for you.
That would make me happy and hopefully you, too.
It would be like starting all over, you see.
Then I could say that eighty is worth every effort
If we could share the next eighty, just you and me.

A He Named ... a She

There was this fella named Stella.
Yes, Stella's dad wanted a girl.
A pretty girl with a big, soft curl.
But when she was born a fella,
Dad still named him Stella.

Years later, Dad noted a beard.
And Stella developed a very deep voice.
And then Dad saw some other things.
By then it was really too late ...
He had named his first son Stella.

Now Stella was an all-right guy.
Some would say a little shy.
But it all came to a head,
When Stella married and went to bed
With a girl named ... Stella.

But Stella, unlike his father before him,
Wanted a boy to be born first but got a girl instead.
But of course, like father like son, he named her ... Fred.
And that's how in folklore it is said,
That Stella and Stella had a girl named Fred.

They also had a dog named Butch,
And to call it a male was pure folly.
For when it went for walk and never headed for a tree,
All the world could certainly see that when it took a _____.
It was a folly not to call him Molly.

Dad or Stella will never ever learn
That gender resides within a name.
They cannot use a name to fulfill their aim.
So when all is done and said.
You probably will never see another Stella or Molly or Fred.

Final Statement

He: "Must you always have the last word?"

She: "No, I don't think so."

He: "Watch."

She: "Okay."

He: "See."

She: "It was not the last word. I said okay. It was only a response to what you said."

He: "Yes, but it is also the last word."

She: "Right!"

He: "See! This is silly. We could do this all night."

She: "Okay, then go to sleep."

She: "Stop. Don't do that."

He: "But you are so appealing."

She: "I know. But not tonight."

He: "You smell so nice."

She: "I know ... but ... no. Stop! I am getting angry."

He: "Do you remember when we were first married?"

She: "Yes. But right now I am trying to forget."

He: "You said you love me."

She: "I do. But that has nothing to do with tonight."

He: (Mumbles.)

She: "Don't do that."

He: "Do what?"

She: "Don't mumble at me."

He: "Well then ..."

She: "No."

He: "See?"

She: "Okay ... I do have the last word."

*P*hoto Gallery — Chapter 7

Top: Memorial Day, Cranford, NJ
Bottom: Early Morning Snow, Springfield Ave.,
Cranford, NJ from the short story "First Bacon."

Top: 9/11 Memorial, Cranford, NJ
Bottom, Left: Industrial Rail, Cranford, NJ
Bottom, Right: Statue of Liberty, New York Harbor, NYC

Top: Red-Tailed Hawk, Cranford, NJ
Bottom: Commuters waiting in the train tunnel
for the NYC bus before 6 a.m. They must all be
asleep because no one talks in the line.

Top: "Shep" from the story "First Bacon" after his morning walk.
Bottom, Left: Orphaned (by an automobile) deer, Cranford, NJ.
Bottom, Right: River Tunnel and reflection, Cranford, NJ.

Top: Lunch time, Turtle Pond, secret location, Kenilworth, NJ.
Bottom, Left: Monmouth Park Race Track, Freehold, NJ.
Bottom, Right: Nomaheagan Park Foot Bridge, Cranford, NJ.

Top: Alaskan train entering tunnel on
White Pass Railway, 1000 feet
above the river (used by gold prospectors during the gold rush)
Bottom: Glacier meeting the sea in Glacier Park, Alaska.

Top: Humpback whale (approx. twenty tons), Alaska.
Bottom, Left: Killer whales (Orcas) feasting on seals; Alaska.
Bottom, Right: Mendenhall Glacer, Juneau, Alaska.

Top: Nomaheagan Park, Cranford, NJ.
Bottom: Hidden home of a ground squirrel, West Orange, NJ

Top: Reflecting lake, Nomahagean Park, Cranford, NJ
Bottom, Left: Red-tailed hawk, Bird Preserve, Kenilworth, NJ
Bottom, Right: Sunset on Pacific en route to Juneau, Alaska

Top: Snow and ice covered mountain peak, Alaska.
Bottom: Margery Glacier calfing (our lucky day), Alaska

Top: Hansen Park and Sperry Dam, Cranford, New Jersey
Bottom, left: Fall meadow and mountain, Alaska
Bottom, right: Glacier, valley, and mountain, Alaska

Top: "Night Workers," award winning photograph, Cranford, NJ.
Bottom: Young deer venturing away from its
mother and father, Kenilworth, NJ.

Top: Beautiful tree with Spanish moss, Charleston, SC.
Bottom: Sunrise over Vancouver Island, Canada.

Above: West Side Highway, above 80th Street, New York City.

Note: All photographs are color, digital, original, copyrighted©, and may be purchased in various sizes by calling John at 908-803-7901 with the photo description.